From Jo March's Attic

From

Jo March's Attic

Stories of Intrigue and Suspense

♦ ♦ ♦ ♦ ♦

LOUISA MAY ALCOTT

Edited by Madeleine B. Stern
and Daniel Shealy

Northeastern University Press
BOSTON

Northeastern University Press

Library of Congress Cataloging-in-Publication Data
Alcott, Louisa May, 1832–1888.
From Jo March's attic : stories of intrigue and suspense / Louisa
May Alcott ; edited by Madeleine B. Stern and Daniel Shealy.
p. cm.
Includes bibliographical references.
Contents: Dr. Dorn's revenge—Countess Varazoff—Fatal follies
—Fate in a fan—Which wins?—Honor's fortune—My mysterious
mademoiselle—Betrayed by a buckle—La Belle Bayadère.
ISBN 1-55553-177-6 (cl)
1. Detective and mystery stories, American. 2. Horror tales, American.   I.
Stern, Madeleine B., 1912–   .   II. Shealy, Daniel.   III. Title.
PS1016.S73   1993
813'.4—dc20   93-25412

ALC

Designed by Diane Levy

Composed in Garamond #3 by Graphic Composition, Inc., Athens,
Georgia. Printed and bound by Thomson-Shore, Inc.,
Dexter, Michigan. The paper is Glatfelter
Offset, an acid-free sheet.

MANUFACTURED IN THE UNITED STATES OF AMERICA
98 97 96 95 94   5 4 3 2

To Victor A. Berch, Literary Detective

Contents

Acknowledgments ix

Introduction xi

Doctor Dorn's Revenge 3

Countess Varazoff 17

Fatal Follies 37

Fate in a Fan 57

Which Wins? 75

Honor's Fortune 93

My Mysterious Mademoiselle 111

Betrayed by a Buckle 127

La Belle Bayadère 145

Bibliography 163

Acknowledgments

IN PREPARING THIS EDITION, we have incurred many debts of gratitude. We are especially grateful to Victor A. Berch, former Special Collections Librarian of Brandeis University, who first located these stories; our debt to him is immeasurable. We are also grateful to the following people for assistance in obtaining copies of the Alcott thrillers: Beth Diefendorf, Rose Chief Librarian, General Research Division, New York Public Library, and Tom Burnett, Reference Librarian, University of Michigan Library. Many thanks also to the Library of Congress and the Boston Public Library for help in locating copies of *Frank Leslie's Lady's Magazine*.

Kristen Hatch first brought this project to the attention of Northeastern University Press; we are grateful for her help and encouragement.

Madeleine B. Stern acknowledges the unceasing support of her partner, Dr. Leona Rostenberg, who originally discovered Alcott's pseudonymous works. Daniel Shealy acknowledges the support of the Department of English at the University of North Carolina–Charlotte. He is also indebted to his parents, Ralph and Ruby Shealy, and to his brothers, Roger and Clayton, for their kind support and encouragement.

Madeleine B. Stern

Introduction

THIS IS THE FIFTH COLLECTION of Alcott thrillers to appear between 1975 and 1993, thrillers whose themes include sexual power struggles, narcotics addiction, murder, revenge, and feminist triumph over the male lords of creation. In the most recent of those collections, *Freaks of Genius,* I stated: "It is certain that there are more such tales concealed in the now crumbling weeklies of the 1850s and the 1860s. It is equally certain that they will remain undiscovered." As it turns out, the first prediction has been proven correct, the second false.

Louisa May Alcott's double literary life was a well-kept secret for almost a century. The sensational narratives she produced in a Boston attic were clandestinely dispatched to the tabloids of her day, where they were devoured by avid readers. But no one knew that those wild and gaudy tales had been written by the author of *Flower Fables* and *Little Women,* for Alcott's ventures into sensationalism were either anonymous or pseudonymous. She did not choose to acknowledge her explorations in the underworld. The nineteenth-century story papers to which she contributed were in her view not on an intellectual or class level with the exalted *Atlantic Monthly,* for example. Of one such story paper she remarked, "No one takes it here [Concord]." [1]

Despite her secrecy, a handful of scholars had suspected, from cryptic entries in her journals and allusions in her letters, that the creator of the wholesome March family had also created characters who delved in evil and traded in darkness. Not until 1943, however, was the suspicion replaced by certainty. Then, in an article entitled "Some Anonymous and Pseudonymous Thrillers of Louisa M. Alcott,"[2] Leona Rostenberg proved beyond a doubt that the spinner of salutary tales for the young had also been the manufacturer of a corpus of quite different narratives. Rostenberg's article, published in a learned periodical, established the fact but did not reprint the stories. It was not until 1975 that a handful of the clandestine narratives that had appeared anonymously or pseudonymously were finally made available to a readership that could revel in their fascinations and marvel that they had been written by America's best-loved author of juveniles.[3]

Although there was no doubt at the time of the high quality of Alcott's sensational tales, there was no firm idea of their quantity. Only in the years that followed was it discovered that she had been as prolific in her output for an adult readership as for her juvenile followers. Alcott had written far more sensation stories than had been supposed. The Boston attic had been a secret manufactory of fascinating fiction.

How, since those stories were unacknowledged and published without her name, were they finally traced? Their identification with Alcott itself forms a bit of a thriller.

Rostenberg based her discovery that Alcott had written sensation stories under a pseudonym—"A. M. Barnard"—upon five letters she found among the Alcott papers at Harvard, letters written in 1865 and 1866 by a Boston publisher, James R. Elliott, to Alcott, requesting "anything in either the sketch or Novelette line that you do not wish to 'father', or that you wish A. M. Barnard. or 'any other man' to be responsible for."[4]

Whether or not Alcott objected to Elliott's use of the word "father" and the phrase "any other man" for her feminist shockers, she produced them with cosmic regularity. Eventually they were collected and published—along with other sensation stories traced to her pen from clues scattered in her letters and journals—as *Behind a Mask, Plots and Counterplots, A Double Life,* and *Freaks of Genius.*

It was Alcott's account books that provided the clues to the hidden thrillers in *From Jo March's Attic.*[5] In those records of her finances, the thrifty Yankee, weaving tales to help support a more or less impoverished family, entered the abbreviated results of her productivity. In the year 1867, for example, she mentioned: "In Oct. took a room in B[oston]. & wrote all winter. . . ." What she wrote and what she earned were listed, and the 1867 list included "Dr Donn. [$]22" and "Countess Irma [$]25."[6] Alcott continued her summation for her climactic year of 1868, when Part One of *Little Women* was published, and that list included "Fatal Follies [$]25" and "Fate In A Fan [$]25."[7] The following year, when she reported she had been "Sick all winter & wrote nothing but little tales," the list was extended with "Which Wins [$]25," "Mademoiselle [$]25," "Honor's Fortune [$]25," as well as "Betrayed" and "La Belle Bayadere," each $25.[8]

Those nine stories were traced to their source—*Frank Leslie's Lady's Magazine*—by still another persistent and insatiable literary detective, the scholar Victor Berch. Knowing him as an avid scanner of popular nineteenth-century American periodicals, and having profited frequently from his unerringly eagle eye, I had provided him with a list of these thus far unlocated titles from Alcott's account books. The results were gratifying. Searching the *Lady's Magazine,* Berch soon matched Alcott's abbreviated entries with stories from its pages.[9] The "Dr Donn" for which Alcott had received $25 appeared there as "Doctor Dorn's Revenge"; "Countess Irma" as "Countess Varazoff," whose first name was Irma; "Mademoiselle" as "My Mysterious Mademoiselle"; "Betrayed" as "Betrayed by a Buckle." The remaining stories had been accurately titled in the writer's account books.

Mr. Berch was facilitated in his search by another brief hint in those account books. In front of the titles "Betrayed" and "La Belle Bayadere" Alcott had written "two stories for 'Leslie.'"[10] The allusion was to Frank Leslie, publishing magnate of the 1860s and 1870s, a titan on New York's Publishers' Row. His empire included a host of weeklies and monthlies, among them *Frank Leslie's Illustrated Newspaper, Frank Leslie's Chimney Corner,* and *Frank Leslie's Lady's Magazine.*

The anonymous effusions written by Alcott for *Leslie's Illustrated Newspaper* and *Chimney Corner* had already been located and anthologized. "Pauline's Passion and Punishment," "A Whisper in the Dark," "A Pair of Eyes," "The Fate of the Forrests," "A Double Tragedy," and "A Nurse's Story," among others, had all been spotted in those Leslie periodicals and reprinted in "unknown thriller" Alcott collections. But it was not until Victor Berch examined the pages of *Frank Leslie's Lady's Magazine* that the stories in the present collection were located. Somehow, the *Lady's Magazine* seemed more a purveyor of fashion than a story paper, and it had not been viewed as a likely vehicle for Alcott's gaudy tales. Now that the previously unlocated titles scribbled in Alcott's account books had been traced to the *Lady's Magazine,* Louisa Alcott emerged as a star contributor to yet another Leslie periodical.

Alcott's relationship with the Frank Leslie Publishing House had begun as early as 1862 and would last till the end of the decade. Besides being a productive relationship, it strengthened her connections with the editor of *Frank Leslie's Lady's Magazine,* a woman named Miriam Squier, who was not only Frank Leslie's editor but his mistress. One day she would become Mrs. Frank Leslie, and later head of the Leslie publishing empire. Miriam Squier had another distinction: she could have sat for the portrait of heroine in the Alcott shockers she was about to publish.[11]

One cannot help wondering whether that industrious scribbler Jo March ever met her editor, or indeed ever actually entered the establishment at 537 Pearl Street, New York City, that housed the Leslie operations. It had become a kind of pictorial factory, a prodigious mail order business, this huge five-story publishing house that eventually hired three hundred to four hundred employees. Alcott visited or passed through New York upon several occasions—on her way to Washington late in 1862, on her way to Europe in 1870, and later on for more extended stays. She loved the warm generosity of New Yorkers and would have relished the opportunity to leave sleepy Concord to confer with a publisher in the metropolis.

If she did so, she would have met the vigorous, black-bearded Frank Leslie, whose lively eyes reflected his dynamic magnetism. Alcott, who had written under a pseudonym, may possibly have known that Frank Leslie lived under a pseudonym, his real name being Henry Carter; and despite her reservations regarding his business methods, she would certainly have been intrigued by his dominant personality. Indeed, the "black-bearded artist Max Erdmann" in her Leslie serial "A Pair of Eyes"[12] bears close resemblance to the black-bearded publisher of pictorial periodicals.

In 1861, Frank Leslie had engaged the archaeologist Ephraim George Squier as editor of the *Illustrated Newspaper* and so had set the stage for the sort of sensational melodrama that his contributor Miss Alcott excelled in. Squier's wife, Miriam, would in the course of her long, eventful life boast four husbands (Leslie would succeed Squier) as well as a number of extramarital conquests, hold sway as a salon leader, and eventually, almost single-handedly, manage the vast Leslie Publishing House. She began her career under the pseudonym of Minnie Montez, so-called sister of the notorious Lola Montez, with whom she made a provincial tour. After Frank Leslie's death she would change her name legally to Frank Leslie and end her career by bequeathing two million dollars to the cause of woman suffrage. Her life was as colorfully plotted as any of Alcott's most garish serials. With her lustrous gray eyes and coppery gold hair she was extraordinarily beautiful. She was also, during the 1860s when Alcott was a Leslie contributor, on her way to becoming a power behind the Leslie throne. As she wrote in an article entitled "Woman's Mission," "When Columbus braved the perils of unknown seas to add America to the world, it was the white hand of a woman that fitted him for his . . . voyage."[13] It was the white hand of Miriam Squier that controlled not only *Frank Leslie's Chimney Corner,* but another periodical that was the perfect vehicle for her particular talents, *Frank Leslie's Lady's Magazine.*

The magazine had already had a long history.[14] Indeed, it had been the first of Leslie's ventures, preceding his *Illustrated Newspaper.* Begun in January 1854 as *Frank Leslie's Ladies Gazette of Fashion,* it had undergone a few changes of name before becoming, in February 1863, *Frank Leslie's Lady's Magazine.* Edited originally by Ann Stephens, author of the first Beadle dime novel, *Malaeska,*[15] the monthly had specialized in "fashionable" as well as "literary" intelligence. Instruction in crochet had vied with stories, national fashions and paper patterns with narratives reflecting "the great talent that exists everywhere among us." Under the aegis of Miriam Squier, Civil War material was dropped from the periodical, such questions as "Is Marriage A Lottery?" were debated, and the most sensational features were toned down for a fairly refined female readership. With descriptions of Mexican mantelets and Ristori corselets, coiffures Creole and coiffures Josephine, the *Lady's Magazine* investigated in minute detail "What Should be Worn and What Should Not," and the popularity of the venture was such that in time it showed a yearly profit of over $39,000.

For this success not only the fashion news was responsible, but the short story featured in each issue. And it was for those stories that the skills of Louisa May Alcott were called upon by the woman who edited the *Lady's Magazine*—a periodical of the women, by the women, and for the women. The direction and scope of the *Lady's Magazine* did not, however, encompass any militant feminism. Rampant feminism in the 1860s was centered upon woman's right to her own being, politically, economically, sexually. Although Alcott occasionally injected such a theme into her narratives for the periodical, it was neither demanded nor expected by editor Miriam Squier. The requirements for contributions to the *Lady's Magazine* reflected the subscriber's attitude toward women as well as the editorial concept of women. Its narratives were tailored to the reader's predilections and to the editor's perception of those predilections. Unlike the serials carried by the *Illustrated Newspaper* and the *Chimney Corner,* the stories in the *Lady's Magazine* were short, seldom covering more than four small quarto pages, two columns to a page—just long enough to be scanned quickly by women readers thumbing pages for advice on mantilla paletots or Minerva coiffures. Since payment depended upon quantity rather than quality, it never rose higher than $25 a story, unlike the $50 or $100 paid for more extended tales. Besides being short, stories carried by the *Lady's Magazine* were characterized for the most part by a kind of modified sensationalism. Violent themes such as narcotics addiction and brutal murder, welcomed by the *Illustrated Newspaper* or the *Chimney Corner,* were here eschewed. The toned-down sensationalism, however, did not preclude the titillations of sexual exchanges or the excitement of sexual power struggles.

In addition, stories in the *Lady's Magazine* were expected to suggest to a Leslie artist a graphic illustration, depicting for example "My husband and your wife" in a curtained alcove, or "Madame senseless on her husband's bosom, as he lay dead and cold upon his bed." Like the writers, the artists were anonymous.

These requirements mirrored not only the standards of editor Miriam Squier but the interests of women readers of the late 1860s. Apparently they were avid for stories that hovered on the fringes of sexual excitement and were not too violently plotted, stories short and easy to read, in which the heroine might be a feminist but must be feminine.

Although no contract between Leslie and Alcott has survived, it is easy enough to reconstruct its terms: $25 for a story of stipulated length and semi-sensational character, to be illustrated and published anonymously every few months. The nine stories that have been traced to Alcott in the *Lady's Magazine* between February 1868 and February 1870 conform to those requirements and presumably were among the reasons for the periodical's success.

Louisa Alcott had little difficulty in fulfilling the demands of editor Miriam Squier. By the years 1867 to 1869, when the stories were written, she had developed the kind of professionalism that could assay the interests of specific readerships and supply them. She had written, and was still writing, for a number of different journals, adapting her skills to their individual needs. Her experience in the 1850s with the very first periodical for which she had been a regular contributor, the Boston *Saturday Evening Gazette,* had taught her to cut the length of a story to editorial requirements. When its editor William Warland Clapp criticized her work, she replied to him on 25 October 1856: "I find it difficult to make them [my stories] interesting & yet short enough to suit your paper. But hope to improve in both points."[16] Her improvement on both scores is notable in her contributions to the *Lady's Magazine.* Alcott's ability to tell a tale, which she could spin out to five installments for serial publication or confine to four pages for appearance in a single issue, is remarkable. Even more so is the author's versatility. It is difficult to understand how, during her productive 1860s, she was writing almost at the same time the militantly feminist sensation story "Behind a Mask; or, A Woman's Power" for the *Flag of Our Union,* the Civil War narrative "The Blue and the Gray, A Hospital Sketch" for *Putnam's Magazine,* a succession of thrillers for *Frank Leslie's Chimney Corner,* children's tales for *Merry's Museum,* which she also edited—and *Little Women!*

Moving between Concord and Boston during those years of intense literary productivity, Alcott was continuously pursued by the family's need for money. To supply coal to warm the Orchard House, boots for her philosopher father, Bronson Alcott, shoes for her long-suffering mother, art lessons for her sister May, comforts for all the family, she appointed herself Alcott breadwinner, and to this end tried every means then available of making money, from teaching to nursing, from domestic service to sewing, and especially, and always, writing.

In 1868, when Alcott was producing "Fatal Follies" and "Fate in a Fan" for *Frank Leslie's Lady's Magazine,* she was also drawing, in the book that would become a perennial classic, her self-portrait, Jo March. Jo, rebellious, as yet untamed, writes in her attic, just as her creator was doing, mild romances for the *Spread Eagle,* sensation stories like "The Duke's Daughter" and "A Phantom Hand" for pictorial story papers, and a novel.

"Every few weeks," we are told in the chapter of *Little Women* entitled "Literary Lessons":

> she [Jo] would shut herself up in her room, put on her scribbling suit, and "fall into a vortex," . . . writing away. . . . Her "scribbling suit" consisted of a black woolen pinafore on which she could wipe her pen at will, and a cap of the same material, adorned with a cheerful red bow, into which she bundled her hair when the decks were cleared for action. This cap was a beacon to the inquiring eyes of her family, who during these periods kept their distance, merely popping in their heads semioccasionally to ask, with interest, "Does genius burn, Jo?"

Surely it was in such an attic room, where Jo March fell into a vortex, that Alcott's varied literary output originated. There she considered the nature of *Frank Leslie's Lady's Magazine,* and there she created protagonists who would act out their roles in melodramatic stories tailored to length for women readers in between their visits to the Sponsalia Millinery Rooms and Madame Rallings' Magasin des Modes.

At this point it should be made clear, however, that the short stories dispatched by Alcott to Miriam Squier for publication in the *Lady's Magazine* were written not after but before she was assured of the success of *Little Women. Little Women,* Part One, was published October 1, 1868; Part Two was not published until April 14, 1869, and it was not until December 25, 1869, that Roberts Brothers sent her the then substantial amount of $2500 in royalties.

The time lag between writing and publication may mislead

some into believing that Alcott was still concocting thrillers for Leslie after she had become the successful author of *Little Women.* It must therefore be pointed out that the composition of the Leslie shockers preceded their actual publication often by months. "Doctor Dorn's Revenge" and "Countess Varazoff" were both written in 1867, before *Little Women* had been begun; "Fatal Follies" was published in September 1868, just before *Little Women,* Part One, appeared. "Fate in a Fan," written in 1868, was published in January 1869, before publication of *Little Women,* Part Two. The remaining five stories in the present collection were all written in 1869, including "Betrayed by a Buckle" and "La Belle Bayadère," which did not see publication until February 1870. Thus, though it may appear that the writing of some of these tales postdated the successful reception of *Little Women,* it did not.[17]

The nine short stories contributed by Alcott to the *Lady's Magazine* before she became America's best-loved author of juvenile fiction were drawn in one way or another from her own life as well as from her readings. Besides attracting subscribers to the *Lady's Magazine* and earning her over $200, they reflect the manner in which the author reshaped her experiences and her imaginings into readable narratives for a specific audience.

The themes woven into the fabric of this fiction stemmed from episodes Alcott had lived or observed.[18] One of those themes, strangely enough, was the plight of Poland. In January 1863, when an insurrection erupted in Warsaw, Alcott was returning from her short stint as Civil War nurse in the Union Hotel Hospital, Georgetown, D.C., and trying to recover from the serious illness she had contracted there. Events in far-off Poland, where Russia was subduing the rebellion but not the surge of nationalism, seemed to have no bearing upon her life. It was not until November 1865 that, traveling abroad as companion to a young invalid, Alcott met, in the enchanting Swiss village of Vevey, a young veteran of that Polish insurrection. Ladislas Wisniewski, age twenty, who had suffered from exposure during the campaign, had been forced to leave his country. The thirty-three-year-old woman from Concord and the delightful young Polish exile were drawn to each other, exchanging lessons not only in English and French, but in the American and Polish rebellions. Reports of Fredericksburg were matched by Ladislas' stories of the Cossack march against Langiewicz. As she treasured his companionship, Alcott found yet another character for her fiction.

In 1867, the year that publisher Thomas Niles of Roberts Brothers asked Alcott to write a girls' book, the prolific author took a room at 6 Hayward Place and "rode to B[oston]. on my load of furniture." There, in what she styled "Gamp's Garret," she would produce *Little Women,* in which the universally loved hero Laurie was modeled in large part upon the young Pole Ladislas Wisniewski. At almost the same time, she was writing a story for the editor of *Frank Leslie's Lady's Magazine* entitled "Countess Varazoff," or, as she entered in her account book, "Countess Irma." Published in June 1868, when Alcott was sending "twelve chapters of 'L.W.' to Mr. N.," "Countess Varazoff" dramatizes a power struggle, sexual and political, between the Polish exile Irma Varazoff and the Russian conqueror Prince Czertski. Although the countess is spirited and vivacious in public, we learn that she is sad in private. And while she mourns her country—"Poland no longer exists"—she smiles upon her enemy, the Russian prince. Sensual, ruthless, courageous, with fierce black eyes and closely cropped black hair, Prince Czertski has "the temper of a demon and the pride of Lucifer." In fact, he closely resembles the Russian hero of yet another Alcott narrative, "Taming a Tartar," [19] where the power struggle ends happily. Here, it does not.

At a *bal masqué*, Irma Varazoff appears in "mourning robes with fettered hands" in the guise of the Genius of Poland, while the Russian prince appears as Peter the Great. And, seemingly, such are their life roles. When the prince assures the countess, "I am your slave," she responds, "My master, rather. It is I who am the slave."

Yet, the ironic ending reverses those roles. Irma Varazoff, as she says, does "not fear. I have nothing more to lose—but my life, and that is a burden I would willingly lay down." Despite her "abhorrence and despair," she marries the Russian conqueror—a union explained by the subplot. She has married him only to obtain a pardon for a compatriot who languishes in an Austrian prison. Once that is accomplished, she is free to deprive her hated husband of his Polish prize, defeating him by her suicide. Her suicide note becomes Alcott's technical device for encapsulating involved answers to previously unanswered questions in a brief note:

> I have kept my promise, and by a month of bitter martyrdom earned my rest. . . . In marrying you, Alexander Czertski, I save my beloved benefactor, and return to you as much as I may of the wrong, the shame, and suffering which you dealt out to my countrymen. I am not a countess, . . . but the child of a serf, freed and tenderly fostered by the old man whom I have saved. To a Russian noble the disgrace of such an alliance as yours is an indelible stain, and knowing this, I married you. . . . Bequeathing this legacy to you, I escape from you for ever. . . .

And so, Alcott's defiant, courageous Polish woman who assumed the guise of the Genius of Poland vindicates her country and herself, and, by her death, triumphs over the Russian conqueror. The struggle between the two graphically drawn protagonists is dramatically conveyed. Ladislas Wisniewski had certainly given the author the inspiration if not the plot for this powerful narrative. Her imagination had done the rest.

The author was not yet done with Polish heroines. Not long after she sent Part Two of *Little Women* to her publisher— wherein Laurie marries not Jo March but her sister Amy—the *Lady's Magazine* published another short anonymous Alcott tale, "Which Wins?" In that extraordinary story, two women are pitted against one another as rival queens: the stately, blonde Austrian Thyra and the slender, vivid Polish Nadine. Their conflict and even its ghastly outcome are, however, of less interest than the narrative's setting. The background of this vengeful thriller happens to be the Paris Exposition of 1867, which had been attended not by Louisa Alcott of Gamp's Garret, Boston, but by her publisher, his star editor, and the editor's husband. The question posed to the literary detective is: Had Alcott heard of their melodramatic visit to the Paris Exposition of 1867 and, if so, had she made use of it in her story? A comparison of the two versions suggests the interesting possibility that the writer had based her sensation narrative, in part at least, upon the one that had actually taken place.

The title of the Leslie-Squier Paris scenario might well have been "Plot and Passion." Since March 1866, Frank Leslie had been regaling his subscribers with details of the forthcoming Paris Universal Exposition. In November he had been appointed a United States commissioner to judge the fine arts exhibits, and, having invited Miriam and E. G. Squier to join him, he sailed abroad in February 1867. A trio was soon to degenerate into a triangle.[20]

E. G. Squier had earlier borrowed, from a source in Liverpool, £350 that he had never repaid. With the malicious intent of an Alcott villain, Frank Leslie notified Squier's creditor of their imminent arrival, induced Squier to land in Liverpool, and there Miriam's unfortunate husband was arrested as an absconding debtor and imprisoned in Lancaster Castle.

Part II of the drama ensued. Leaving Squier in prison, Miriam and Leslie journeyed to London, where the publisher borrowed £350 for Squier's release, but postponed handing the sum over until he and Miriam had enjoyed London to the full. Finally, having posted bail, Leslie continued on to Paris with his two editors.

Paris in the Exposition year of 1867 danced *en fête.* The Exposition opened April 1, and before Miriam Squier's eyes there unfolded a panorama of exotic costumes worn by a carnival of crowned heads led by that high priestess of crinoline, the Empress Eugénie. While Leslie, with Squier's help, prepared his *Report on the Fine Arts,* Miriam meditated upon the Paris fashions that she would describe for subscribers to her *Lady's Magazine.* The state ball at the Tuileries honoring the czar of Russia crowned the imperial fêtes before the trio journeyed on to Italy.

It is hard to believe that Louisa Alcott had not heard some gossip about this tumultuous trio at the Paris Exposition and incorporated bits of it into her story for the *Lady's Magazine.* "Which Wins?" contains several points of comparison with the Leslie adventure: the Exposition background, including the distribution of prizes at the Palace of Industry; an important episode concerning the choice of costumes worn by the protagonists at a *bal masqué;* and finally the disclosure that the count whom the Viennese Thyra hoped to wed was really a convict. If those details of plot and passion struck Miriam Squier as suspiciously suggestive of her own experiences in Paris, she did not allow the possibility to interfere with the story's publication in her periodical, where "Which Wins?" appeared in March 1869.

Subscribers doubtless devoured the descriptions of costumes, the revelation that the count was a convict, and especially the terrible, vengeful finale in which Thyra contrived the disfigurement of her rival, Nadine:

> . . . One end of Nadine's mantilla had blown out among the leaves that rustled in the wind; some peeping servant had left a half-smoked cigarette on the balcony, . . . Thyra saw a way to avenge her wrongs, and prove herself the victor. . . . It was the work of an instant to lift the smoldering spark and lay it on the filmy fabric, to watch the breeze fan it to a little flame, and the flame steal on unobserved till the mantilla suddenly blazed up like an awful glory about the fair head of its wearer. . . .
> "Disfigured for life! disfigured for life!"

Exercising her limitless imagination along with her tireless pen, and using bits and pieces from hearsay, observation, or her own life, Alcott kept up a steady flow of short, wild tales for the *Lady's Magazine.*

"Fate in a Fan," published in January 1869, is a shocker revolving about gambling. Its major prop is a white lace fan, owned by the lovely Leontine, which serves as a weapon. The pearl and gold handle holds "a slender crystal vial," and when its spring stopper is touched it exudes a "subtle Indian perfume" that intoxicates and stupefies. The treacherous fan is used to dull the senses of her father's opponents at the gaming table, but "this artful toy" plays an even more baleful role.

One of the primary points of interest about "Fate in a Fan" is the fact that the fan is manipulated by Leontine at the command of her father, St. Pierre. Was the author perhaps recalling Hawthorne's famous story "Rappaccini's Daughter," in which Beatrice is transformed by her scientific father into a kind of poison carrier? Or, rather, was the relationship between daughter and father in Alcott's shocker based in some way upon the relationship between Louisa and Bronson Alcott? That relationship has long been the subject of considerable speculation among Alcott scholars. Louisa's attitude toward her father was complicated, compounded of pride in his philosophical and pedagogical accomplishments and impatience with his inability to earn money. Did her love-hate, admiration-depreciation feelings play any part in the Leontine–St. Pierre relationship? Perhaps they formed a sediment for the hatred felt for her father by the heroine of "Fate in a Fan."

St. Pierre, who had learned the secret of the fan when he served as a soldier in the East, commands his daughter to use it as a weapon to ruin a hated gambling opponent. The "delicious drowsiness" it produces is comparable with the "heavenly drowsiness" from hashish in the Alcott thriller "Perilous Play,"[21] published only a month later than "Fate in a Fan" in another Leslie story paper. Leontine acts as "a puppet in her father's hand," until, finally, she reveals her hostility in a passionate outburst: "I will confess all, but oh, save me from my father!. . . I dread him more than death. . . . The poison is killing me by inches, but I dared not rebel. . . . My father . . . had the fan made as if for a harmless odor, and forced me to use it with that horrible stuff hidden in it. I sit by his opponents when he plays, and . . . my treacherous fan dulls their senses, and my father plunders them."

As Leontine realizes, the fan is actually killing *her,* a process she hastens by drinking the poison and ending her "blighted life." By combining an aromatic toxin with a cruel gambling father, Alcott created a neat short thriller for the *Lady's Magazine,* and at the same time doubtless worked off any hidden animosity she may have harbored for Bronson Alcott.

From time to time, Alcott wove into her sensation stories preoccupations less domestic than exotic, as in her use of details of Hindu life. Her serial "The Fate of the Forrests," published in 1865 in *Leslie's Illustrated Newspaper,* was based upon the atrocity of Hindu Thuggism.[22] The poison in "Fate in a Fan" was Indian. Even in such an innocent little tale as "Honor's Fortune"—a paean to virtue rewarded—the author injected an Indian touch, her hero inheriting a fortune from Uncle Hugh who "went away to India." Still more pronounced are the Hindu embellishments that heighten the exotic nature of that feminist narrative "La Belle Bayadère," embellishments that stem less from episodes of Alcott's life than from her reading.

The British role in India was certainly a popular topic in the 1860s, and the Leslie journals themselves featured from time to time delectable descriptions of Indian customs. Indeed, in the very issue of the *Lady's Magazine* that ran the anonymous Alcott effusion "Betrayed by a Buckle," there was a paragraph headed "Hindoos Exhibiting Learned Birds." In 1869, when she wrote "La Belle Bayadère," she could appropriate from an arsenal of sources those "souvenirs of India" that enrich the story.

Some of those "souvenirs" are projected onto a stage where an Indian prince is portrayed on a tiger hunt, and his mate, representing the "Spirit of the Ganges," suggests the eternal joys of a Hindu paradise. As for the bayadère herself, that vengeful, triumphant heroine is depicted as not only an entrancing dancer but "a true Hindoo," for "none but a true Hindoo would have remembered the *khol* on the eyelids, the *henna* on the finger-tips, the gauzy *tab* over the bosom, or worn bangles with such ease, and dared attempt to dance with bare feet."

The tale dominated by the belle bayadère is one of man's perfidy and woman's revenge. The treacherous Englishman Philip Cope had loved the bayadère in India—or feigned love—and now, when the dancer reappears upon a western stage, she avenges his past betrayal and "subjugates" him to her will.

Introduction

Readers of the *Lady's Magazine* were doubtless enthralled not only by the story but by its Hindu appurtenances, and especially by the bayadère herself, whose dancing was "fire and force, no leap too daring, no step too intricate," whose abandon surely transported not only her own audience, but Alcott's too.

Everything was grist for the writer's mill, and the thrillers that flowed from Jo March's attic were drawn from Alcott's life, from her readings, and even from her dreams. Sometimes, as during her convalescence from the typhoid-pneumonia suffered during her period of Civil War nursing, those dreams were nightmares. In January 1863 she confided to her journal:

> As I never shall forget the strange fancies that haunted me I shall amuse myself with recording some of them. The most vivid & enduring was a conviction that I had married a stout, handsome Spaniard, dressed in black velvet with eery soft hands & a voice that was continually saying, "Lie still, my dear." This was mother, I suspect, but with all the comfort I often found in her presence there was blended an awful fear of the Spanish spouse who was always coming after me, appearing out of closets, in at windows, or t[h]reatening me dreadfully all night long.[23]

Alcott never did forget those "strange fancies," and, writing compulsively for Leslie journals later in the decade, put them to fictional use. "Fatal Follies," written and published in Alcott's productive year of 1868, is an unusual tale that hinges upon the theme of repetitive dreams and monomania. It is a story of love and loathing between husband and wife who suspect each other of murderous instincts toward each other. The suspicions are grounded in dreams, dreams of poisoning and destruction. As the attending doctor thinks, "Great heavens, what an unhappy mania for self-torture these children possess. . . . Are both mad? or which is sane!" Poison, suicide, and a broken heart dramatically punctuate this short shocker for a lady's magazine distilled by Jo March from the psychology of nightmarish dreams.

A still more provocative psychological ingredient was stirred into the broth of "My Mysterious Mademoiselle." Written in 1869, the year Part Two of *Little Women* was published, it presents, in a way, a Jo March in reverse. Jo, as one critic has aptly put it, was—and is—"the tomboy dream come true,"[24] the reflection of an author who "never liked girls or knew many, except my sisters,"[25] under whose bib and tucker a boy's heart beat loud and strong. Many of those boyish or tomboyish attributes were imparted to Jo March, helping to make her the fiery, independent spirit who dominated and still dominates *Little Women.*

In "My Mysterious Mademoiselle" Alcott indulged in a kind of reverse portrait, presenting her young hero in the disguise of a girl. The result is a delicious trifle which, despite the innocent explanations of the denouement, must convey to the twentieth-century reader certain transvestite suggestions. Some of them are highly titillating. An Englishman—a "big, black-bearded gentleman"—meets on a train "a slender girl of sixteen or so," a "demure demoiselle," who informs him that she is "helpless." After kissing her hand "in true French style," he begins, as he confesses in this first-person narrative, "to find my school-girl a most captivating companion. . . . I felt blithe and young again, for my lost love seemed to sit beside me; I forgot my years, and almost fancied myself an ardent lad again. . . . I enjoyed the little adventure without a thought of consequences." "The idea of passing as her father disgusted me," he confides, "and I preferred a more youthful title."

For a time, the Englishman pretends the young girl is his wife, and she promises to give him "anything." When they part, he asks her to give him "an English good-by," that is, "a kiss on the lips." He has observed the mademoiselle when, believing him asleep, she takes his flask of wine and a chocolate croquette, and, in no ladylike fashion, drinks and eats. "Poor little thing," he thinks, "she is hungry, cold, and tired; . . . She is far too young and pretty to be traveling alone. I must take care of her."

As it turns out, the mysterious mademoiselle is in disguise. The young lady is really a "handsome, black-haired, mischievous lad" who has transformed himself to escape his school authorities. As he explains, "Often at school I have played girl-parts, because I am small, and have as yet no beard." With the aid of a blonde wig, a little rouge, a soft tone, a modest air, he has become a "mademoiselle." [26] By Alcottian coincidence, the two protagonists, it is disclosed, are related, and presumably nephew and uncle will in future enjoy a perfectly normal and natural relationship. Meanwhile, the tale, which must have surprised and delighted nineteenth-century readers, may raise a few eyebrows today.

With two additional narratives—"Doctor Dorn's Revenge," a tale of retribution for the mercenary marital choice made by a woman, and "Betrayed by a Buckle," the portrait of an evil woman and her punishment—the author of *Little Women* has achieved yet another fascinating collection of sensation stories. Written, as they were, for a woman editor, and published in a woman's magazine, they naturally emphasize the role of woman in situations marked by conflict and passion. Yet they avoid the extremes of violence, brutal murder, and narcotics addiction that are pivotal in other Alcott sensation stories devised for more general readerships. There is much of the melodramatic left here, in the way of poison and suicide, vengeance and retribution, titillating sex and even transvestite suggestions, to make of these narratives fast and good reads. As one would expect, there is considerable emphasis upon fashion, costume often playing a focal part, as in "Countess Varazoff." While the feminism interwoven in the stories is seldom rampantly militant, it is nonetheless present almost throughout.

These tales elucidate the author's shaping of sources into fiction, reflect the complexities of her literary imagination, extend her productivity. Best of all, the nine anonymous narratives that flowed from Jo March's attic continue to intrigue. These short, sweet shockers of the 1860s are short, sweet shockers today.

A Note on the Text

IN PREPARING THESE STORIES for publication, we have made silent emendations only where the text would be obviously in error or unclear without them. For example, we have corrected obvious spelling and typographical errors, inserted words and punctuation for clarity, and provided single or double quotation marks where they were missing. We have let stand nineteenth-century spellings and inconsistencies in capitalization. Alcott was often careless in preparing her manuscripts for publication, and compositors for nineteenth-century newspapers and magazines were not particularly careful in setting type from even the best-prepared copy. In general, we have tried to modernize or "correct" the text as little as possible.

Notes

1. Louisa May Alcott to James Redpath, 28 August [1863], in *The Selected Letters of Louisa May Alcott,* ed. Joel Myerson, Daniel Shealy, Madeleine B. Stern (Boston: Little, Brown, 1987), p. 89 (hereafter cited as *Selected Letters*).

2. Leona Rostenberg, "Some Anonymous and Pseudonymous Thrillers of Louisa M. Alcott," *Papers of the Bibliographical Society of America* 37 (2d Quarter, 1943).

3. Madeleine B. Stern, ed., *Behind a Mask: The Unknown Thrillers of Louisa May Alcott* (New York: William Morrow, 1975).

4. James R. Elliott to Louisa May Alcott, 5, 7, 21 January, 15 June 1865, and August 1866 (Louisa May Alcott MSS., Houghton Library, Harvard University).

5. Alcott's account book entries appear as "Notes and Memoranda" in *The Journals of Louisa May Alcott,* ed. Joel Myerson, Daniel Shealy, Madeleine B. Stern (Boston: Little, Brown, 1989) (hereafter cited as *Journals*).

6. *Journals,* p. 159.

7. *Journals,* p. 168.

8. *Journals,* pp. 172, 173n.10.

9. When, years before, in connection with my biography of Mrs. Frank Leslie, I had examined *Frank Leslie's Lady's Magazine,* I was unaware of the story titles in Alcott's account books. My indebtedness to Victor Berch of Marlboro, Mass., former Special Collections Librarian of Brandeis University, cannot be exaggerated.

10. *Journals,* 173n.10.

11. For Miriam Squier and the Leslie publishing empire, see Madeleine B. Stern, *Purple Passage: The Life of Mrs. Frank Leslie* (Norman: University of Oklahoma Press, 1970).

12. "A Pair of Eyes; or, Modern Magic," *Frank Leslie's Illustrated Newspaper* (24 and 31 October 1863).

13. "Woman's Mission," *Frank Leslie's Lady's Magazine* (December 1877), p. 447. See Stern, *Purple Passage,* p. 78.

14. See Stern, *Purple Passage,* pp. 39–40, 189, 197–198, 217–218; Madeleine B. Stern, *We the Women: Career Firsts of Nineteenth-Century America* (New York: Schulte, 1963), p. 38.

15. In 1860 the New York firm of Irwin P. Beadle launched the first dime novel series with the publication of Ann Stephens's *Malaeska.*

16. *Selected Letters,* p. 18. See also Madeleine B. Stern, "Louisa May Alcott and the Boston *Saturday Evening Gazette*," *American Periodicals* (Fall 1992).

17. There is the further possibility that some of the stories listed as sold during 1867–1869 had actually been written prior to the year in which they were accepted.
18. For details of Alcott's life, see Madeleine B. Stern, *Louisa May Alcott* (Norman: University of Oklahoma Press, 1985).
19. "Taming a Tartar," *Frank Leslie's Illustrated Newspaper* (30 November and 7, 14, 21 December 1867).
20. For details, see Stern, *Purple Passage,* pp. 47–51, 220–222.
21. "Perilous Play," *Frank Leslie's Chimney Corner* (13 February 1869).
22. "The Fate of the Forrests," *Frank Leslie's Illustrated Newspaper* (11, 18, 25 February 1865). Hindu Thuggism was the barbarous practice by professional assassins and worshippers of the Hindu goddess of destruction; they strangled and plundered their victims as a religious duty. The practice was eradicated by the British during the nineteenth century.
23. *Journals,* p. 116. For other instance of the effect of these nightmares, see Madeleine B. Stern, ed., *Plots and Counterplots: More Unknown Thrillers of Louisa May Alcott* (New York: William Morrow, 1976), pp. 9–10.
24. Elizabeth Janeway, "Meg, Jo, Beth, Amy and Louisa," reprinted from the *New York Times Book Review* (27 September 1968) in Madeleine B. Stern, ed., *Critical Essays on Louisa May Alcott* (Boston: G. K. Hall, 1984), pp. 97–98.
25. *Journals,* pp. 165–166.
26. For other instances of Alcott's use of her fascination with the stage, see Stern, ed., *Behind a Mask,* pp. xi, xviii–xix, and Madeleine B. Stern, Joel Myerson, and Daniel Shealy, eds., *A Double Life: Newly Discovered Thrillers of Louisa May Alcott* (Boston: Little, Brown, 1988), pp. 15–17.

From Jo March's Attic

Doctor Dorn's Revenge

THEY STOOD TOGETHER by the sea, and it was evident the old, old story was being told, for the man's face was full of pale excitement, the girl's half averted from the ardent eyes that strove to read the fateful answer in her own.

"It may be folly to speak when I have so little to offer," he said, with an accent of strong and tender emotion in his voice that went straight to the girl's heart. "It may be folly, and yet if you love as I love we can wait or work together happy in the affection which wealth cannot buy nor poverty destroy. Tell me truly, Evelyn, may I hope?"

She longed to say "yes," for in her heart she knew she loved this man, so rich in youth, comeliness, talent, and ardor, but, alas! so poor in fortune and friends, power and place. He possessed all that wins a woman's eye and heart, nothing that gratifies worldly ambition or the vanity that is satisfied with luxury regardless of love. She was young, proud, and poor, her beauty was her only gift, and she saw in it her only means of attaining the place she coveted. She had no hope but in a wealthy marriage; for this end she lived and wrought, and had almost won it, when Max Dorn appeared, and for the first time her heart rebelled. Something in the manful courage, the patient endurance with which he met and bore, and would in time conquer misfortune, woke her admiration and respect. He was different from those about her, and carried with him the unconscious but sovereign charm of integrity. The love she saw in his eloquent eyes seemed a different passion from the shallow, selfish sentimentality of other men. It seemed to ennoble by its sincerity, to bless by its tenderness, and she found it hard to put it by.

As she listened to his brief appeal, made impressive by the intensity of repressed feeling that trembled in it, she wavered, hesitated, and tried to silence conscience by a false plea of duty. Half turning with the shy glance, the soft flush of maiden love and shame, she said slowly:

"If I answered yes I should wrong both of us, for while you work and I wait that this may be made possible, our youth and strength will be passing away, and when the end is won we shall be old and tired, and even love itself worn out."

"If it be true love it never can wear out," he cried, impetuously; but she shook her delicate head, and a shadow passed across her charming face, paling its bloom and saddening its beauty.

"I know that poets say so, but I have no faith in the belief. Hearts grow gray as well as heads, and love cannot defy time any more than youth can. I've seen it tried and it always fails."

"So young, yet so worldly-wise, so lovely, yet so doubtful of love's dominion," murmured Max, on whom her words fell with a foreboding chill.

"I have felt the bitterness of poverty, and it has made me old before my time," she answered, with the shadow deepening on her face. "I could love you, but—I will not." And the red lips closed resolutely as the hard words left them.

"Because I am poor?"

"Because *we* are poor."

For an instant something like contempt shone in his eyes,

then pity softened their dark brilliance, and a passionate pain thrilled his voice as he said, with a despairing glance:

"Then I may not hope!"

She could not utter the cruel word "No" that rose to her lips; a sudden impulse ruled her; the better nature she had tried to kill prompted a truer answer, and love, half against her will, replied:

"You may hope—a little longer."

"How long?" he questioned, almost sternly, for even with the joy of hope came a vague disquiet and distrust.

"Till to-morrow."

The tell-tale color flushed into her cheeks as the words escaped her, and she could not meet the keen yet tender eyes that searched her downcast face.

"To-morrow!" he echoed; "that is a short probation, but none the less hard for its brevity if I read your face aright. John Meredith has spoken, and you find money more tempting than love."

Her head dropped on her hands, and for an instant she struggled with an almost irresistible impulse to put her hand in his and show him she was nobler than he believed. But she had been taught to control natural impulses, to bend her will, to yield her freedom to the one aim of her life, and calling it necessity, to become its slave. Something in his look and tone stung her pride and gave her strength to fight against her heart. In one thing he was mistaken; John Meredith had not spoken, but she knew a glance from her would unlock his tongue, for the prize was almost won, and nothing but this sudden secret love had withheld her from seizing the fruit of her long labor and desire. She meant to assure herself of this beyond all doubt, and then, when both fates were possible, to weigh and decide as calmly as she might. To this purpose she clung, and lifting her head with a proud gesture, she said, in the cold, hard tone that jarred upon his ear and made discord in the music of her voice:

"You need not wait until to-morrow. Will you receive your answer now?"

"No; I will be patient, for I know something of temptations like this, and I have faith in the nobility of a woman's heart. Love or leave me as you will, but, Evelyn, if you value your own peace, if you care for the reverence of one who loves you utterly, do not sell yourself, for wealth so bought is worse than the sharpest poverty. A word will put me out of pain; think of this to-day; wear these to remind you of me, as that jewel recalls Meredith; and to-night return my dead roses or give me one yourself."

He put the ruddy cluster in the hand that wore his rival's gift, looked into her face with a world of love and longing in his proud eyes, and left her there alone.

If he had seen her crush the roses on her lips and drench them in passionate tears, if he had heard her breathe his name in tones of tenderest grief and call him back to save her from temptation, he would have turned and spared himself a lifelong loss, and saved her from a sacrifice that doomed her to remorse. She crept into a shadowy nook among the rocks, and searched herself as she had never done before. The desire to be found worthy of him swayed her strongly, and almost conquered the beliefs and purposes of her whole life. An hour passed, and with an expression more beautiful than any ever seen upon her face till now, Evelyn rose to seek and tell her lover that she could not give his flowers back.

As she stood a moment smiling down upon the emblems of love, a voice marred the happiest instant of her life, a single sentence undid the work of that thoughtful hour.

"Meredith will never marry pretty Evelyn."

"And why not?" returned another voice, as careless as that sarcastic one that spoke first.

"He is too wise, and she lacks skill. My faith! with half her beauty I would have conquered a dozen such as he."

"You have a more potent charm than beauty, for wealth will buy any man."

"Not all." And the girl's keen ear detected an undertone of bitterness in the light laugh that followed the words. A woman spoke, and as she listened, Dorn's words, "I know something of such temptations," returned to her with a sudden significance which the next words confirmed.

"Ah, Max will not thaw under your smiles nor be dazzled by the golden baits you offer. Well, my dear, you can find your revenge in watching Evelyn's folly and its dreary consequences, for she will marry him and ruin herself for ever."

"No doubt of that; she hasn't wit enough to see what a splendid career is open to her if she marries Meredith, and she will let a girlish romance rob her of success. That knowledge is an immense comfort to me."

The speakers passed on, leaving Evelyn pale with anger, her eyes keen and hard, her lips smiling scornfully, and her heart full of bitterness. The roses lay at her feet, and the hand that wore the ring was clinched as she watched mother and daughter stroll away, little dreaming that their worldly gossip had roused the girl's worst passions and given her temptation double force.

"She loves Max and pities me—good! I'll let her know that I refused him, and teach her to fear as well as envy me. 'A splendid career'—and she thinks I'll lose it. Wait a day and see if I have not wit enough to know it, and skill enough to secure it. 'Girlish romance' shall not ruin my future; I see its folly, and I thank that woman for showing me how to avoid it. Take comfort while you may, false friend; to-morrow your punishment will begin."

Snatching up the roses, Evelyn returned to the hotel, congratulating herself that she had not spoken hastily and pledged her word to Dorn. Everything seemed to foster the purpose that had wavered for an hour, and even trifles lent their weight to turn the scale in favor of the mercenary choice. As if conscious of the struggle going on within her, Meredith forgot the temporary jealousy of Dorn, that had held him aloof for a time, and was more devoted than before. She drove with him, and leaning in his luxurious barouche, passed Dorn walking through the dust. A momentary pang smote her as his face kindled when he saw her, but she conquered it by whispering to herself, "That woman would rejoice to see me walking there beside him; now I can eclipse her even in so small a thing as this."

As the thought came, her haughty little head rose erect, her eye wandered, well pleased, from splendid horses, liveried servants and emblazoned carriage, to the man who could make them hers, and she smiled on him with a glance that touched the cold heart which she alone had ever warmed.

Later, as she sat among a group of summer friends, listening to their gossip, she covertly watched her two lovers while she stored up the hints, opinions, and criticisms of those about her. Max Dorn had youth, manly beauty and native dignity, but lacked that indescribable something which marks the polished man of fashion, and by dress, manner, speech and attitude betrayed that he was outside the charmed circle as plainly as if a visible barrier rose between him and his rival.

John Meredith, a cold, grave man of forty, bore the mark of patrician birth and breeding in every feature, tone, and act. Not handsome, graceful, or gifted, but simply an aristocrat in pride and position as in purse. Men envied, imitated, and feared him; women courted, flattered, and sighed for him; and whomsoever he married would be, in spite of herself, a queen of society.

As she watched him the girl's purpose strengthened, for on no one did his eye linger as on herself; every mark of his preference raised her in the estimation of her mates, and already was she beginning to feel the intoxicating power which would be wholly hers if she accepted him.

"I will!" she said, within herself. "To-night he will speak and to-morrow my brilliant future shall begin."

As she dressed for the ball that night an exquisite bouquet of exotics was brought her. She knew who sent them, and a glance of gratified vanity went from the flowers to the lovely head they would adorn. In a glass on her toilet bloomed the wild roses, fresh and fragrant as ever. A regretful sigh escaped her as she took them up, saying softly, "I must return them, but he'll soon forget—and so shall I."

A thorn pierced her hand as she spoke, and as if daunted by the omen, she paused an instant while tears of mental, not physical pain, filled her eyes. She wiped the tiny drop of blood from her white palm, and as she did so the flash of the diamond caught her eye. A quick change passed over her, and dashing away the tears, she hid the wound and followed her chaperon, looking blithe and beautiful as ever.

John Meredith did speak that night, and Max Dorn knew it, for his eye never left the little figure with the wild roses half hidden in the lace that stirred with the beating of the girlish heart he coveted. He saw them pass into the moonlit garden, and stood like a sentinel at the gate till a glimmer of white foretold their return. Evelyn's face he could not see, for she averted it, and turned from the crowd as if to seek her room

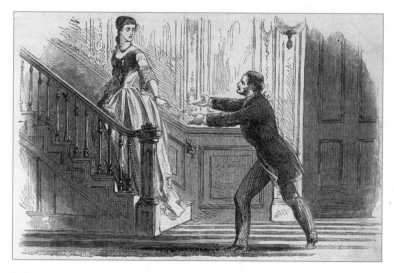

"No one was near, and pausing, she turned to look down on him."

unseen. Meredith's pale features were slightly flushed, and his cold eye shone with unwonted fire, but whether anger or joy wrought the change Dorn could not tell.

Hurrying after Evelyn, he saw her half way up the wide staircase, and softly called her name. No one was near, and pausing, she turned to look down on him. Never had she seemed more lovely, yet never had he found it hard to watch that beloved face before. Without a word he looked up, and stretched his hands to her, as if unconscious of the distance between them. Her rich color faded, her lips trembled, but her eyes did not fall before his own, and her hand went steadily to her breast as in silence, more bitterly significant than words, she dropped the dead roses at his feet.

Dr. Dorn's Revenge

Is DOCTOR DORN AT HOME?"

The servant glanced from the pale, eager speaker to the elegant carriage he had left, and, though past the hour, admitted him.

A room, perfect in the taste and fitness of its furnishing, and betraying many evidences, not only of the wealth, but the cultivation of its owner, received the new comer, who glanced hastily about him as he advanced toward its occupant, who bent over a desk writing rapidly.

"Doctor Dorn, can you spare me a few moments on a case of life and death?" said the gentleman, in an imploring tone, for the sight of a line of carriages outside, and a crowded anteroom inside, had impressed him with the skill and success of this doctor more deeply than all the tales he had heard of his marvelous powers.

Doctor Dorn glanced at his watch.

"I can give you exactly five minutes."

"Thanks. Then let me as briefly as possible tell you the case. My wife is dying with a tumor in the side. I have tried everything, every physician, and all in vain. I should have applied to you long ago, had not Evelyn positively forbid it."

As the words left his lips both men looked at one another, with the memory of that summer night ten years ago rising freshly before them. John Meredith's cold face flushed with emotion in speaking of his suffering wife to the man who had been his rival. But Max Dorn's pale, impassive countenance never changed a muscle, though a close observer might have seen a momentary gleam of something like satisfaction in his dark eye as he answered in a perfectly business-like tone:

"I have heard of Mrs. Meredith's case from Doctor Savant, and know the particulars. Will you name your wish?"

He knew it already, but he would not spare this man the

pang of asking his wife's life at his hands. Meredith moistened his dry lips, and answered slowly:

"They tell me an operation may save her, and she consents. Doctor Savant dares not undertake it, and says no one but you can do it. Can you? Will you?"

"But Mrs. Meredith forbids it."

"She is to be deceived; your name is not to be mentioned; and she is to think Doctor Savant is the man."

A bitter smile touched Dorn's lips, as he replied with significant emphasis:

"I decline to undertake the case at this late stage. Savant will do his best faithfully, and I hope will succeed. Good morning, sir."

Meredith turned proudly away, and Dorn bent over his writing. But at the door the husband paused, for the thought of his lovely young wife dying for want of this man's skill rent his heart and bowed his spirit. With an impulsive gesture he retraced his steps, saying brokenly:

"Doctor Dorn, I beseech you to revoke that answer. Forgive the past, save my Evelyn, and make me your debtor for life. All the honor shall be yours; she will bless you, and I—I will thank you, serve you, love you to my dying day."

Hard and cold as stone was Dorn's face as the other spoke, and for a moment no answer came. Meredith's imploring eyes saw no relenting sign, his outstretched hands fell at his side, and grief, resentment and despair trembled in his voice as he said, solemnly:

"For her sake I humbled myself to plead with you, believing you a nobler man than you have proved yourself. She took your heart, you take her life, for no hand but yours can save her. You might have won our gratitude forever, but you refused."

"I consent." And with a look that went straight to the other's heart, Dorn held out his hand.

Meredith wrung it silently, and the first tears that had wet his eyes for years fell on the generous hand that gave him back his idol's life.

The affair was rapidly arranged, and as no time was to be lost, the following day was fixed. Evelyn was to be kept in ignorance of Dorn's part in the matter, and Doctor Savant was to prepare everything as if he were to be the operator. Dorn was not to appear till she was unconscious, and she was not to be told to whom she owed her life till she was out of danger.

The hour came, and Dorn was shown into the chamber, where on the narrow table Evelyn lay, white and unconscious, as if dead. Savant, and two other physicians, anxious to see the great surgeon at work, stood near; and Meredith hung over the beautiful woman as if it was impossible to yield her up to them. As he entered the room Dorn snatched one hungry glance at the beloved face, and tore his eyes away, saying to the nurse who came to him, "Cover her face."

The woman began to question him, but Meredith understood, and with his own hands laid a delicate handkerchief over the pallid face. Then he withdrew to an alcove, and behind the curtain prayed with heart and soul for the salvation of the one creature whom he loved.

The examination and consultation over, Dorn turned to take up his knife. As he did so one of the physicians whispered to the other, with a sneer:

"See his hand tremble; mine is steadier than that."

"He is as pale as the sheet; it's my opinion that his success is owing to lucky accidents more than to skill or science," returned the other.

In the dead silence of the room, the least whisper was audible. Dorn flushed to the forehead, he set his teeth, nerved his arm, and with a clear, calm eye, and unfaltering hand made the first incision in the white flesh, dearer to him than his own.

It was a strange, nay, an almost awful sight, that luxurious room, and in the full glow of the noonday light that beautiful white figure, with four pale men bending over it, watching with breathless interest the movements of one skillful pair of hands moving among the glittering instruments or delicately tying arteries, severing nerves, and gliding heedfully among vital organs, where a hair's-breadth slip might be death. And looking from behind the curtains, a haggard countenance full of anguish, hope and suspense.

With speechless wonder and admiration the three followed Dorn through the intricacies of this complicated operation, envying the steadiness of his hand, firm as iron, yet delicate as a breath; watching the precision of his strokes, the success of his treatment, and most of all, admiring his entire absorption in the work; his utter forgetfulness of the subject, whose youth and beauty might well unnerve the most skillful hand. No sign of what he suffered during that brief time escaped him; but when all was safely over, and Evelyn lay again in her bed, great drops stood upon his forehead, and as Meredith grasped his hand he found it cold as stone. To the praises of his rivals in science, and the fervent thanks of his rival in love, he returned scarce any answer, and with careful directions to the nurse went away to fall faint and exhausted on his bed, crying with the tearless love and longing of a man, "Oh, my darling, I have saved you only to lose you again!—only to give you up to a fate harder for me to bear than death."

Evelyn lived, and when she learned to whom she owed her life, she covered her face, saying to her hungry heart, "If he had known how utterly weary I was, how empty my life, how remorseful my conscience, he would have let me die."

She had learned long ago the folly of her choice, and pined in her splendid home for Max, and love and poverty again. He had prospered wonderfully, for the energy that was as native to him as his fidelity, led him to labor for ambition's sake when love was denied him. Devoted to his profession, he lived on that alone, and in ten years won a brilliant success. Honor, wealth, position were his now, and any woman might have been proud to share his lot. But none were wooed; and in his distant home he watched over Evelyn unseen, unknown—and loved her still.

She had tasted the full bitterness of her fate, had repented and striven to atone by devoting herself to Meredith, who was unalterable in his passion for her. But his love and her devotion could not bring happiness, and when he died his parting words were, "Now you are free."

She reproached herself for the thrill of joy that came as she listened, and whispered penitently, "Forgive me, I was not worthy of such love." For a year she mourned for him sincerely; but she was young, she loved with a woman's fervor now, and hope would paint a happy future with Max.

He never wrote nor came, and wearying at last, she sent a letter to a friend in that distant city, asking news of Doctor Dorn. The answer brought small comfort, for it told her that an epidemic had broken out, and that the first to volunteer for the most dangerous post was Max Dorn.

In a moment her decision was taken. "I must be near him; I must save him—if it is not too late. He must not sacrifice himself; he would not be so reckless if he knew that any one cared for him."

Telling no one of her purpose, she left her solitary home and went to find her lover, regardless of danger. The city was deserted by all but the wretched poor and the busy middle class, who live by daily labor. She heard from many lips praises, blessings and prayers when she uttered Doctor Dorn's name, but it was not so easy to find him. He was never at home, but lived in hospitals, and the haunts of suffering day and night. She wrote and sent to him. No answer came. She visited his house to find it empty. She grew desperate, and went to seek for him where few dared venture, and here she learned that he had been missing for three days. Her heart stood still, for many dropped, died, and were buried hastily, leaving no name behind them. Regardless of everything but the desire to find him, dead or living, she plunged into the most infected quarter of the town, and after hours of sights and sounds that haunted her for years, she found him.

In a poor woman's room, nursed as tenderly by her and the child he had saved as if he had been her son, lay Max, dying. He was past help now, unconscious, and out of pain, and as she sat beside him, heart-stricken and despairing, Evelyn received her punishment for the act which wrecked her own life and led his to an end like that.

As if her presence dimly impressed his failing senses, a smile broke over his pallid lips, his hand feebly groped for hers, and those magnificent eyes of his shone unclouded for a moment, as she whispered remorsefully:

"I loved you best; forgive me, Max, and tell me you remember Evelyn."

"You said I might hope a little longer; I'll be patient, dear, and wait."

And with the words he was gone, leaving her twice widowed.

Countess Varazoff

Chapter I

Bonjour, monsieur vane. I am consumed with curiosity to learn who the blonde angel is yonder."

"Countess Irma Varazoff," replied the young Englishman, turning to meet the tall Russian who accosted him somewhat imperiously.

Both paused to look after one of the charming little vehicles which fly up and down the Promenade des Anglais at five P.M. in the height of the season at Nice. It was lined with blue silk as daintily as a lady's work-basket, ornamented by a handsome page in the little seat behind, drawn by snow-white ponies in silver-plated harness and blue favors, and driven by a lovely young woman, whose costume of blue velvet and ermine completed the coquettish *tout ensemble*. "Who is she?" asked the Russian as they went on.

"A Polish widow, lately arrived here."

"You mistake, *mon ami;* she is a Russian; Poland no longer exists. You know her, and you will present me, if I ask the favor?"

"Would it be generous to present the conqueror to the conquered?"

"Bah! what have charming women to do with such things; if one admires them they are satisfied," returned the Russian, carelessly.

"Not if the admirer has robbed them of country, friends, and fortune. Some women do not forget," said Vane, ill-pleased.

"They are soon taught that lesson. Is the countess one of these proud rebels?"

"She does me the honor to be my friend, and I cannot offend her by complying with your wish. Indeed it is impossible," and the cool decision of the young Englishman left no hope.

"I ask no more, but permit me to assure you that the word 'impossible' is unknown to me. With thanks for your complaisance I go to salute the beautiful countess."

As he spoke, with an ironical bow, and a significant smile, the Russian passed on, wearing a look which justified the rumor that Prince Czertski never forgot nor forgave a slight.

He was a man of forty, above the usual height, with a martial carriage, a colorless, large-featured face, fierce black eyes, a sensual, yet ruthless mouth, closely cropped black hair, sharp white teeth under a heavy mustache, and delicately gloved hands as small as a woman's. Dressed with an elegant simplicity, and wearing one order at his buttonhole, the prince was a striking figure, even in the brilliant crowd on the promenade.

Both men walked on, a few paces apart, both angry and both ready to annoy each other. The carriage of the countess was seen returning, and both hastened to reach the opening in the blooming hedge which separated promenade from drive, for it was evident that the lady was about to alight. The prince had the advantage and kept it. With no appearance of haste, he emerged from between the roses just as the countess alighted, and in doing so dropped a coral-tipped white parasol. The little page was evidently new to the duties of his place, for he left his mistress to disentangle her train from the step while he held the horses. With the easy gallantry of a foreigner the prince stepped forward and assisted her, taking care to crush the delicate handle of the parasol under his heel. Then affecting to perceive the accident, he caught it up, exclaiming, with well-feigned regret:

"A thousand pardons for my *gaucherie!* Madame will permit me to repair my fault. To what address shall I send this when it is restored?"

"It is nothing; monsieur need not incommode himself," and the countess extended her hand to reclaim her property. At this moment Vane, who had been detained by a countrywoman, came up, and the prince, with a triumphant glance, said, in a tone of relief:

"Behold my friend, who is known to madame; he will assure her that I may be trusted with this costly toy."

There was no help for it, and Vane presented him with an ill-grace; this chagrin changed to astonishment, however, for, as he uttered the name of one of Poland's most inveterate enemies, he thought to see the countess betray some sign of emotion; but no, the smile remained unchanged, and her beautiful eyes met tranquilly the glance of undisguised admiration bent upon her.

"I could have believed it of any woman but Irma," he muttered to himself, as the countess walked on, speaking without a shadow of annoyance to the prince, who sauntered beside her wearing his most bland and brilliant smile.

Down the long promenade they went side by side, followed by many eyes and criticised by many tongues. Vane hardly spoke, for the prince absorbed the conversation, and when he chose no one could be more charming. The grace and devotion of his manner to women was doubly flattering from its strong contrast to his brusque and domineering demeanor with his own sex. To most women there was a singular fascination in seeing the fierce eyes soften, the pale, impassive face flush and kindle, and the hard mouth smile as it uttered honeyed compliments or impassioned vows.

Countess Varazoff observed him with furtive glances as if to catch every change of feature, to weigh every word he uttered; and during that careless interview she appeared to be testing the man by some subtle process of her own. Her conclusions were evidently favorable, for her manner became more and more gracious, and when the prince quitted them her fine eyes followed him thoughtfully.

"Have no fears for your parasol; madame, it will return to you with a point lace cover and a jeweled handle; these barbarians love magnificence," said Vane, annoyed by her interest in another.

"You fancy I think of that trifle? One day you will know me better," and the countess turned from him with a sombre smile.

Chapter II

A̤LL THE WORLD was at the consul's *bal masqué* three weeks later, and all the world gossiped about Prince Czertski and the Countess Varazoff.

"My dear creature, she will get him," whispered one dowager to another as they watched the brilliant crowd from the gallery. "His carriage waits at her door by the hour together, her anteroom is supplied by the flowers he sends, and he follows her everywhere like a shadow."

"It is true; he adores her and she permits it, yet my son assures me that not a breath of scandal has touched her name. Another week, they say, will show us one of two miracles, the prince rejected or the lovely Pole the wife of the ugly Russian," returned the other old lady, nodding wisely.

"She is as peculiar as she is beautiful. My friend, Madame Cartozzi, has a maid who formerly lived with the countess, and the girl says she was the saddest creature ever seen—in private, mind you—in public she was then as now all spirit and vivacity. Justine says she often walked her room all night weeping, and the next day would make a splendid toilet and lead the life of a butterfly. It is not wonderful that she mourns her country; but it is mysterious that she smiles on an enemy like the prince."

"He is fabulously rich, my dear, and she must be poor compared to him; he has rank, and hers is nothing but an empty sound now; he has power, and she has not a particle beyond that which her beauty gives her. She will dry her tears and marry him, there is no doubt of that."

"It will be a spectacle, that wedding; and yet I pity her, for they say the prince has the temper of a demon and the pride of Lucifer. She will find herself a slave in golden chains. Apropos of chains, they say she intends to appear to-night as the Genius of Poland, in mourning robes with fettered hands."

"She will scarcely dare to do that with so many Russians and Austrians present," cried the second dowager anxiously.

"She has the courage of a lion if all the tales are true, and for that same reason she will appear before her enemies in the dress I tell you of. See, the prince has stood near the door this half hour waiting for her. I know him by the splendor of his dress. He personates Peter the Great, and does it well, as one may see. But look! she is coming—and yes, she is in black. Great heavens, this grows exciting!" and the two old ladies peered over the balcony with breathless interest.

It *was* the countess, shrouded from head to foot in black

crape; her golden hair falling in loose curls upon her shoulders, and her white arms adorned with a light silver chain from wrist to wrist. Never had she looked more beautiful, for through the vail her skin was dazzlingly fair, her eyes shone large and lustrous as stars, her lips were proud and unsmiling, and in her carriage there was a haughty grace which plainly proved that her free spirit was still unsubdued. She leaned upon the arm of a Red Cross Knight, in whom Vane was easily recognizable. As they made their way through the crowd, a murmur followed them, for this was the sensation of the evening. The impressible French and warm-hearted English felt the pathos of the thing, but the Russians and Austrians saw in it only an insult, which irritated them even while they affected to ignore it. The prince knit his heavy brows and swore a Russian oath in his beard as he watched the slender black figure.

"What whim is this?" he muttered. "Why does she annoy me to-night, when I most wished to do her honor and show the world I am about to triumph? Is it a trial of her power over me? or is it merely womanly bravado? We shall see. I shall not yet commit myself."

He kept aloof, but looked and listened carefully as he roamed from group to group. It soon became apparent that something was wrong, for after the first stir of surprise, admiration and conjecture, a scarcely perceptible cloud seemed to overshadow the company. Frowns, shakes of the head, angry or anxious glances were seen, whispered jests, criticisms, even threats circulated rapidly, and a general impression prevailed that the countess would suffer for her freak. Certain high personages were afraid of offending other high personages by countenancing such an act, and presently a rumor flew about that the beautiful Pole was to be informed of her offense and requested to retire.

"What a mortification that will be," cried one lady to another, as the hint reached her. "If I dared I would warn her, that by retiring at once she might spare herself this disgrace. Surely some friend should tell her she has gone too far. She would be eternally grateful for such a kindness."

"Thanks for the word, madame," said the prince to himself, as he passed the fair speaker with a glance that caused her to maintain for ever after that Prince Czertski had magnificent eyes.

Countess Irma sat in one of the alcoves that opened on the garden, enjoying the fresher air after her slow passage through the saloons. For a moment she was alone, Vane being gone for her mantle. Leaning her head on her hand, she sat looking with absent eyes on the glittering sea below. Her vail was thrown back and the moonlight shone full upon her lovely face, which looked almost stern in its pale immobility. A shadow fell across the light, and turning her head, she saw the prince regarding her with an expression rarely seen upon his face, an expression of pity, touched with some warmer emotion. But his voice was cold and quiet, and his manner distant as he said, glancing over his shoulder to assure himself that they were alone:

"Will madame forgive me if I incur her displeasure by bringing unwelcome news, and believe that I do it in order to spare her the pain of hearing them from less respectful lips?"

"I thank you; pray speak," she answered, with no sign of surprise or interest.

"It is with great reluctance that I obey, but time presses, and I could not resist the impulse which sent me to you in the moment of trouble. Madame's costume has given offense to certain powerful persons, who cannot forgive anything to beauty in misfortune. It is whispered that Madame la Countess will be requested to withdraw, and I hastened to spare her the public insult by suggesting that she leave at once, and do me the honor of accepting my carriage if her own is not in attendance."

She had watched him keenly as he spoke, and in her face he read contempt, defiance, and undaunted courage, but overpowering these strong emotions he saw surprise, gratitude, and something akin to admiration at his act.

"And it is *you* who come to warn and protect me when others fall away?" she said, slowly, looking up at him with the glitter of a tear in her steadfast eyes.

"It is I who venture to prove in act what I have often betrayed by look. Of what use is power if not to protect the weak and innocent?" returned the prince, mildly.

"You are a generous enemy," murmured the countess, evidently touched.

"I am an ardent lover."

"Ah, no; you forget I am an exile, homeless, friendless, countryless, and you——" she paused, with a gesture of her fettered hands more eloquent than words.

"I only remember that you are beautiful, and that *I* love you. Madame, come into the garden for a moment; there we shall be uninterrupted. No breath of air shall chill you. See, the Czar is proud to lend his cloak to cover such shoulders;" and rapidly divesting himself of a short sable-lined pelisse, he laid it about her, and led her away with an air of soft command impossible to resist.

Pacing slowly in the moonlight among the orange-trees and through a wilderness of roses, the prince continued in a tenderer tone, with his hand on the delicate one upon his arm, and his eyes, full of passionate admiration, looking down into her own:

"Madame, others may condemn your act this night and attempt to punish it by banishment; but to me it is a brave deed, and I adore courage even in an—nay, I'll not say enemy; that you can never have the cruelty to be to me. The misfortunes of your country should not be visited too heavily on you, and this harmless tribute to poor Poland should be allowed to pass with pity and respect. You shall not suffer for it, I pledge you my word."

"I do not fear. I have nothing more to lose—but my life, and that is a burden I would willingly lay down."

She spoke bitterly, and a mortal sadness seemed to consume her. For a moment the prince eyed her keenly, then smiled to himself, and said in a lighter tone:

"In making others happy one finds happiness they say; can I not persuade you to try it? We are told to love our enemies; I find it an easy task. Can nothing tempt you to do the same? Madame, you cannot feign ignorance of my passion; I have confessed it in many ways, but never won a sign of hope in return. Ah, let me earn the privilege of protecting you always, as I have the delight of doing now. Put me out of pain, I beseech you," and he bent to read her face.

"I have made no sign, because I have no hope to give. Accept my thanks, and pardon me if I inflict pain where I owe gratitude."

Not a vestige of emotion on her face, the weariness of which piqued him more than the slight emphasis on the word "if." "She doubts me still, or loves Vane," he thought, and glowed with wrath at the idea. Very coldly he bowed, and very proudly he answered:

"Then nothing remains for me but to lead you to a carriage. Our appearance together will quiet the gossips and secure you from further annoyance. I possess power, and for you I do not hesitate to use it."

The last words struck her, she walked in silence a few steps, then looked up with a smile so sudden, so brilliant, that it almost startled him. Leaning more confidingly on his arm, the countess said softly:

"Ah, yes, and you use it so kindly. Pardon my seeming ingratitude, and let me tell you why I refuse the honor you would do me. May I, dare I speak?"

Few men could have refused anything asked in such a voice and accompanied by such a gesture of appeal, such a glance of almost tender longing. The prince yielded to the charm without an effort, and replied impetuously, as he lifted the appealing hand to his lips:

"You may dare anything with me. I am your slave."

"My master, rather. It is I who am the slave, but my fetters are not heavy now." And her eye went from his enamored face to the silver chain which he had involuntarily gathered up as they walked.

"You own it then? You confess that you love me, and permit me to hope?" he cried, seizing both hands in his own.

"I confess my weakness, but I do not yield. I must not, till my work is done, for I have vowed to remain a widow while he suffers."

"He! who?" demanded the prince, fiercely.

"Nay, fear nothing; it is an old man, and no lover," answered the countess, with a laugh that would have sounded unnatural to a less excited listener. Still looking up with the enchanting smile on her lips, the half timid, half tender light in her eyes, and both hands folded on his arm, she continued in a charming tone of confidence which flattered the ruling passion of the prince:

"My friend, that jealousy proves that you love me; I no longer doubt, but will permit the sweet truth to comfort me in the sacrifice I must make. Listen, and help me as only one so powerful, so pitiful can. The old Count Cremlin languishes in an Austrian prison. He was kind to me in my orphaned youth, and I

"Still looking up with the enchanting smile on her lips, she continued in a charming tone of confidence which flattered the ruling passion of the prince."

am grateful. He cries to me for help, and I am powerless. He is harmless, feeble, and poor. He desires only to reach England and die free. But he is forgotten, for he has neither friends, influence, or money. You have all; one line of yours secures his liberty, I send him safely to his daughter, and then——"

"Ah! And then, madame?" broke in the prince, pausing to receive the reply.

"And then I thank you," she said, offering both hands with a look that stirred the prince to his heart's core.

"You give me this?" he demanded, while his pale face flushed and his eye kindled as he crushed one of the soft hands in his eager grasp.

"It is not worthy; but place the old count's pardon there, and it is yours."

The words fell slowly from lips that grew white in uttering

them, but her eye met his steadily. Something in her manner disquieted him, for the fire of his own love made him quick to feel the lack of it in her.

"She is wily and will escape me; I am on my guard, but will win her at all costs and punish her coldness afterward," he thought, and answered with a smile that chilled her to the heart:

"When my ring is on this hand I place the pardon in it. You agree to this, my charming captive?"

"But why wait? Why keep the old man in his pain till we———?" the word "marry" died on her lips, and her eyes fell, lest she should see the feverish eagerness in them.

"I am right," he thought; "she plays for a precious stake, and must play high if she wins. She tries to dupe me with false tenderness. Good! She shall atone for that by finding that my love and hate go hand-in-hand."

This knowledge added zest to his pursuit and stimulated his purpose to succeed in spite of all obstacles. The cruel mouth still wore a smile, but in the bland voice there was a mocking undertone.

"He shall not wait long, this poor old man; and while I bestir myself to procure his pardon you will make ready for the marriage. It must be soon, for I am recalled, and dare not linger."

"When?" she murmured, in a half audible voice.

"Before the month is out I must be in St. Petersburgh. Come, I have a fancy to make a little bargain with you. I promise to give you this pardon the moment you are mine."

"You do not trust me then?" she said, flashing a look at him.

He laughed, and answered with an air of gallant submission, "I know your fair and fickle sex too well to trust them till they are won; then I am blindly devoted. Shall it be as I say, my Irma!"

"Yes."

The little word cost a heroic effort, but though uttered bravely, she shivered and shrunk from his embrace, and tried to conceal behind her vail the abhorrence and despair written on her face. He felt and saw it all, and set his teeth with a grim smile as he led her on, pale and mute as the statues round them. On re-entering the alcove a mirror confronted her; struck by her own pallor, she steeled herself to meet the curious world, and assuming a gay air, she resolved to play her part well at any cost. A feverish color rose to her cheek, excitement lent her eyes new brilliancy, and the desperation of her heart supplied her with a vivacity that charmed all beholders. Throwing back her vail, she arranged her bright hair with effect, and turning to the prince, she said, with an air of coquetry which he had never seen before:

"Now, my Alexander, I am ready to accompany you in your triumphal march."

"How! you know my name and make it sweet by uttering it in such a tone?" cried the prince, delighted and surprised by the new change.

"I did not know it, but it suits you, and it pleases me to play your captive to-night. God knows I am one," she added low to herself as the prince threw on his cloak again.

"Come, then, let me show them that it is no longer possible to annoy or condemn the countess Varazoff. Now you may defy the world, for in my eyes you are my wife."

With a superb air of protection he laid her hand upon his arm and led her away, listening well pleased to the soft clank of the silver chain she wore.

Chapter III

THE FREAK OF THE LOVELY COUNTESS was entirely forgotten next day in the excitement caused by the announcement of her approaching marriage with the prince. The fashionable world was enchanted with the romance of the match, and the promised splendors of the wedding, for the prince seemed bent on doing honor to his choice. To the surprise of those who knew her best, Irma threw herself into the affair with an interest entirely foreign to her character. An intense longing for excitement seemed to possess her, and her devotion to the new task left her no time for reflection, except at night. How those hours were spent none knew, but had any watched her narrowly they would have seen with what terrible rapidity she wasted with the devouring anxiety that mastered her.

On the night before the wedding she sent for Vane, and abruptly asked if he would do a service for which she would bless him forever. He eagerly consented, and she added, with an earnestness that haunted him long afterward:

"You are loyal and brave. I need a stanch friend, and I choose you. To-morrow the one gift I value will be the pardon of an old man. I have told you of him and of the price I pay for his liberty. I desire to be sure that I do not pay it in vain; I trust no one but you. I wish to give you the order for his release, and to know that you will see him safe with his children. Will you do this?"

"I will."

"The instant I place the order in your hands, hasten to do your work, and the hour that Count Cremlin lands in England telegraph to me. I may depend on you for speed, secrecy, and fidelity?"

"You may."

"God bless you! Think kindly of me, and when you hear of those who suffered and died for Poland, remember Irma Varazoff."

"Died! suffered! Surely you do not speak of yourself—you, a happy bride?" exclaimed Vane, seized with an ominous misgiving.

"Happy!" she echoed, in a tone of anguish, as she wrung her hands. "Hush! let me tell one living soul why I suffer, and leave one truthful tongue to defend me when I am gone."

"Gone where?"

"We go to St. Petersburgh, you know," she answered, with a shudder, as if the icy winds of the north already chilled her blood. Leaning nearer, with one hand clutching at his sleeve, and her wild eyes on the door, she whispered, "I swore never to forget my country's wrongs, but to avenge them if I could. I am very weak; but one tyrant's heart shall ache, one proud spirit be humbled, and I will free my good old benefactor before I am satisfied. Then I care little what comes. Others suffer and die for their country, I suffer and live. I am ambitious to excel other martyrs, and I shall, for Austrian prisons, Siberia, and the knout itself, are less terrible than life with this man."

"Good God! and yet you marry him?" cried Vane, fearing her mind was touched by past sorrows.

"Yes, and by that bitter sacrifice I pay the great debt of gratitude I owe Count Cremlin, and avenge, as far as I dare, the wrongs he has suffered."

"But how? You will not commit a crime like Corday or——"

"No, I shall not kill him, but I shall rob him of that which he values more than life. Ask me no more. I must be calm for the morrow. When all is over and I give you the precious paper, you shall know more. Now go, my one true friend, pray for me, and serve me faithfully."

He left her, fearing some tragedy that night, but in the morning saw her at the altar calm and fair as the marble image of a bride. The Russian chapel was a brilliant scene that day, and the splendor of the prince's hotel furnished the world with matter for a nine days' gossip. He seemed a proud and happy man, though few guessed the secret thorn that vexed his soul. No one saw the pale bride shrink as the ring went on, no one heard the stern bridegroom whisper "Mine!" as he led her away, and no one dreamed what a strange little scene took place as they stood together in the glittering saloon before a single guest arrived.

"Now the pardon," she said, abruptly, as she turned to him with haggard eyes and outstretched hand.

"You do not trust me then?" he said, echoing her words with a bitter accent, though he smiled on her like an indulgent master.

"I trust where I am trusted. See, my promise is kept; now fulfill your own," and she pointed to the ring on the hand that trembled with impatience.

"Behold it, but before I give it I deserve my reward. Embrace me, my wife."

One hand held the precious paper, the other drew her close as if bent on subduing the rebellious spirit that still unconsciously betrayed itself. One instant she wavered, and her proud eyes defied him; but it was too late for repentance, the prize was not yet won, and with a sudden effort she completed her hard task. As one soft arm encircled his neck the other secured the pardon, and with a kiss as light and cold as a snow-flake she vanished like a white wraith from the room.

Straight to Vane she hurried, for he was waiting, ready to depart when the word came, like a loyal knight as he was.

"Quick!" she cried, "to horse and away! Lose no time, for every hour is an eternity to me till I learn that the old man is safe."

"I am off, and will do your errand if it costs me my life. But you?—what is it? Your lips bleed and you pant like a hunted deer. Who has troubled you?" demanded Vane, still tortured with vague fears for her.

"It is nothing; my lips belied my heart and I struck them. Go, go!" But as she spoke she clung to him as if her last hope would vanish when he went.

Yielding to an uncontrollable impulse, he whispered passionately:

"Irma, let me stay and save you from this fate?"

"No, it is too late; it could never be; I am——" and she breathed the rest into his ear.

"But for that you would have loved me and let me comfort you? Oh, why doubt me, why fear that I should care for this, and so let me lose you?" he cried reproachfully, though his face changed as he listened.

For an instant they stood reading love and despair in each other's woeful eyes, then, as a bell rang loudly, Vane held the beloved creature close, kissed the wounded lips that did not now belie her heart, and tore himself away for ever.

Their honeymoon was waning, and the prince was beginning to believe that he had married a snow-image, not a mortal woman, when the pale statue suddenly woke and warmed. An English letter came, and as she read it the first tears her husband had ever seen her shed flowed freely, while she clasped her hands, murmuring with fervent gratitude:

"He is safe, my debt is paid, and I am free!"

"Who is this who wrings tears from the eyes of my marble

princess?" asked Czertski, with a suspicious glance at the letter.

She gave it, and having read, he crushed it, saying, with a glance that would have daunted any other woman:

"You loved this man?"

"I do love him. I gave you my hand according to the bond; my heart was already his. Rest easy, I shall never see him again, and you are my master."

So quietly, so coldly she spoke, that the prince found no words to answer her, but with set teeth, clinched hands, and a face full of the pale wrath more terrible than any violent outbreak, he left her to ponder what punishment was due for such perfidy.

With strange eagerness Irma wrote and dispatched several letters, walked through the apartments that had been a splendid prison to her, and on the threshold of the last turned with a gesture of farewell. She never re-entered them, for when her husband sought her she was gone. Reproach and anger, pain and captivity were over, and he found the beautiful pale statue lying dead in her chamber with this letter in her hand:

"I have kept my promise, and by a month of bitter martyrdom earned my rest. The instant that I am assured of Count Cremlin's safety I break my chain and pass to eternal liberty. In marrying you, Alexander Czertski, I save my beloved benefactor, and return to you as much as I may of the wrong, the shame, and suffering which you dealt out to my countrymen. I am not a countess, a widow, or a gentlewoman, but the child of a serf, freed and tenderly fostered by the old man whom I have saved. To a Russian noble the disgrace of such an alliance as yours is an indelible stain, and knowing this, I married you. There is no cure for such a wound, and your proud heart will writhe under this blemish on the name and honor you hold dearer than life. It cannot be hidden, for the story, told as I alone can tell it, and bearing my name, is already sent abroad to fill the world with pity for me, contempt for you, and obloquy for both. Bequeathing this legacy to you, I escape from you for ever, knowing that I leave one true and tender friend to defend my memory and tell the tragedy of my short life."

Fatal Follies

Monsieur le docteur! Monsieur le Docteur, come at once. Madame de Normande has fainted with fatigue, and we cannot restore her. *Mon Dieu!* it is fortunate that you are here, for Doctor Jumal is leagues away!" cried Madame Bentolet, the hostess of the "Petit Corporal," as she rushed into the room where I sat resting myself after a long stroll.

Throwing away my cigar I followed at once, and in the little parlor below found my new patient. A traveling-carriage stood at the door, with every sign of having been hastily deserted, and on the couch lay a very lovely woman, supported in the arms of a young man, who was hanging over her with an expression of such intense anxiety and tenderness, that I felt assured he was her lover or husband. As I advanced he looked up, showing me a singularly attractive face, full of power and passion, and a strange shadow of melancholy, which even the excitement of the moment could not banish.

The lady was pale as marble, and apparently unconscious, but the moment I examined her I perceived that her attack was not of a dangerous nature. Her hand was warm, her pulse strong, though irregular, and her lips as rosy as a child's. Her heart beat rapidly, and as I bent to touch her forehead I saw her eyelids flutter as if about to unclose.

"Speak to her, monsieur; she is recovering," I said, with an odd fancy that the lady was affecting insensibility for some reason or other.

"Leonie, it is I, Louis; speak to me, I implore you," murmured the young man, kissing the pale cheek resting on his shoulder.

A faint color flushed it as if those ardent lips had warmed the snow, and a sigh escaped her, but no word.

"Rest tranquil, madame is conscious, and will soon be herself again. I find no symptoms of exhaustion or suffering."

As I uttered the words my patient opened a pair of soft violet eyes and fixed them on me with a curious expression. In them I fancied I read annoyance, surprise, and reproach; but they passed to that other face, and with a quick, wistful glance fell again, as she said, faintly, "It is nothing. Let us go on."

The instant I said, "Madame is conscious," a change passed over the young man. He started, checked some eager word already on his lips, and gently laying the fair head on the pillow, stepped a little aside, assuming a calm, cool expression, so utterly unlike his former one, that I could not restrain a glance of astonishment.

"A few moments of repose and a glass of wine, will restore madame sufficiently to continue her journey, unless she *is* suffering," I added, as a spasm of pain contracted her white forehead.

"I always suffer, and for me there is no help," she murmured bitterly.

"May I ask madame's malady?"

"My heart—a ceaseless pain there, and no rest," she answered, fixing on me eyes that darkened and dilated with something like despair.

Startled and touched by the sudden energy of her tone, the

sad fact she confided to me, I took her hand, and assuming the fatherly air, which my gray hairs and her youth made permissible, I said, gently, "If my experience and skill can serve you, command them freely my child."

She glanced at the card I offered by way of introducing myself, and as she read the name, she half rose, exclaiming eagerly, "Doctor Baptiste Velsor! I have heard of you, of your skill, your success, your benevolence; I searched for you in Paris, but you were gone, and now I find you here. Surely heaven sent you to me." And, to my infinite surprise, she clung to my hand like one in sore need of help. Before I could speak, she asked, in the same eager tone, "You will serve me? I want you very much. Give me a little time at least."

"I am at madame's orders. My holiday is not yet over, and my time is my own."

"Good! Then you can come with us to the chateau, a league distant? You can give me your advice, your help, for in you I have entire confidence. My friends assure me that Doctor Velsor works miracles, and now I will prove it."

I could only smile, and bow, and turning suddenly to the silent gentleman beside me, she asked, with as peculiar a change in her manner as I had marked in his, "You will permit this, Louis? I desire it so much."

He eyed her keenly, and her color faded, leaving her as pale as when I saw her first, but her imploring glance did not fall, and she clasped her hands as if pleading for a great boon. A slight smile softened the firmly cut mouth as he turned to me, with the easy grace of one born to bestow favors, and said, cordially, "If Monsieur le Docteur will pardon us for spoiling his holiday, I shall rejoice in securing his invaluable services for madame, my wife, and Chateau Normande will be honored by so famous a guest."

"You do me too much honor; I am merely a traveler now, and scarcely in fit order to join a gay circle of summer visitors." I began apologetically, for the dress and equipage of the young pair bore the unmistakable stamp of rank and wealth.

"You will see no one; Louis and I are to be there alone— quite alone." And as she spoke an irrepressible shudder passed through Madame Normande's slender frame.

"There is something amiss here, I am interested in this peculiar couple; I am tired of aimless lounging and may do some good, therefore I'll go," I said to myself; and when the young man again urged me, I consented to accompany them at once, and pass a few days in studying the new case so unexpectedly put into my hands.

Madame sat silent behind her vail as we drove toward the chateau, but, as if my presence was a relief to him, my host seemed to shake off his melancholy and exert himself to entertain me.

It was late when we arrived, and pleading fatigue, madame left us to dine alone, begging me, however, to see her before I slept. Chateau Normande was a charming nest of beauty and luxury, a perfect honeymoon home, and old as I was, I enjoyed the romance of the place and its inhabitants. The more I saw of my host, the more interested I became in him, for to my quick eye, it was evident that there was a worm in the bud of this young man's life, prosperous as it seemed. He talked well and wittily on the various subjects that came up, and appeared to enjoy my society, though now and then I detected a slight absence of mind, caught an uneasy, wandering glance, or observed an abrupt pause, as if he listened for some expected sound. No sign of the former melancholy appeared till the conversation fell upon dreams, then I remarked, that as he questioned me or listened intently to the facts I gave him, the same gloomy shadow stole over him which had struck me at first. I tried to change the subject, but he clung to it pertinaciously, till the lateness of the hour reminded me that madame was waiting. As I spoke of this, his manner changed, and with almost startling abruptness he said, arresting me as I rose to leave him, "Have you had experiences in cases of monomania?"

"Many."

"And have you been successful in curing them?"

"Very successful. I have made this a careful study, and take great interest in it."

"Grant me one moment. Have you ever had a case of a person who was possessed to injure the creature most beloved?"

As he breathed the hurried question into my ear, with pale lips and a tragical glance of his fine black eyes, a sudden suspicion of his sanity flashed over me. This was the shadow on his life, this the cause of his young wife's heartache, and the shudder which passed over her as she spoke of their being alone together, and this the secret of their eagerness to secure my services. A sincere pity filled my soul, and laying my hand on his shoulder, I said, earnestly, "My friend, I am an old man, and have kept many secrets in my life. Confide in me, speak freely, and rest assured that your confidence shall be kept sacred. What afflicts you and your lovely wife? Be frank with me, and let me help you."

Tears filled those handsome eyes of his, and for a moment he seemed to struggle with some strong emotion. But second thoughts evidently counselled caution, and controlling himself, he said, gratefully, "Thanks, you are truly kind. We do need help, and I will confide to you all I dare of the sorrow which oppresses me. It wrings my heart to utter the words, but, hoping all things from your skill, I ask you to watch my wife——"

"Your wife!" I interrupted, in surprise. "Is *she* the mono-maniac of whom you speak?"

"Hush! Yes, it is she," he whispered, with such an expression of deep pain, of entire conviction, that I relinquished my first suspicion at once. "Listen," he continued, regarding me with the sad composure of one who has nerved himself to a hard task, for my exclamation betrayed my mistake to him, and he forgot reserve in the natural desire to clear himself from the suspicion of unsoundness. "We have been married six months, we love each other, we possess all that should make life blest, and yet we are wretched. I saw Leonie but three or four times before we were married, as the affair was arranged between our families. I was heart free, she was lovely, and I felt sure that happiness would follow our union. I was warned, but paid no heed to the warning; I married her, and my honeymoon was scarcely over when I discovered that, with all her seeming love, my wife de-sired to destroy me."

"*Mon Dieu,* how horrible! But are you sure of this? Have you proof? May it not be a mistake, a jealous delusion? My dear Monsieur Normande, what led you to cherish this awful fear?"

Drawing me to a secluded recess, where it was impossible to be overheard, the unhappy young man poured his story into my ear.

"As a physician trusted and honored by many, I confide my secret to your keeping, and as a man of honor I implore you to guard it from the world," he said; and I gave him my hand with the desired promise. "Do you believe in dreams?" was the abrupt question that followed.

"In a measure, as I have told you. But I am not superstitious."

"I am; it runs in our blood, and the dreams of our family have more than once been fatally fulfilled. The week before my wedding I had a dream so vivid that it is still before me, as distinctly as that picture on the wall. I dreamed that I stood in the great *salon* below, and saw advancing toward me the slender figure of a woman clothed in white. Her face was hidden by a vail, under which I caught the gleam of bright hair, but nothing more. In one hand she carried a little casket of ebony and silver, in the other a silver cup like one of those on the table yonder. Gliding up to me, she offered me the cup with an inviting gesture, and I drank. Instantly a horrible pain assailed me, and the figure vanished with a mocking laugh as I fell to the ground, and woke trembling with a strange terror."

"Nightmare, my friend," I began, smiling.

"Listen, there is more," he continued, in the same agitated voice, and glancing behind him with a nervous gesture. "A week after my marriage I dreamed the same dream, more vivid than before, with this difference, that as the phantom vanished it put up its hand, as if to lift the vail, and on that lovely hand I saw the likeness of the wedding ring Leonie wore. A peculiar ring, an heirloom worn by many brides of our house, and never allowed to pass from the family. Observe it when you visit her. Ah, you smile at me and think me a superstitious fool! Wait a little. I told no one of my dreams, but could not forget them, for they haunted me, and disturbed my peace. Just at that time I fancied a change in Leonie. She had begun to love me I felt sure, for I devoted my life to her, and her timidity seemed fast yielding to confidence and affection. She grew sad at times, seemed oppressed with some hidden care or grief; watched me narrowly, shunned me, received my caresses with coldness or tears, and drove me half distracted by her changeful spirits. I bore with it patiently, hoping to win her to a happier mood, but it naturally affected me, and unconsciously our peace was marred by this new and nameless trouble. No entreaties could draw from her a word regarding it, and she turned from me to the gayeties of Paris, as if striving to forget herself and me. This annoyed me, the breach widened, and I was miserable, till a new discovery completed my despair." He paused, went to the table and emptied a glass of wine, wiped his damp forehead, and returning, continued rapidly, "A third time I dreamed the dream, and this time the phantom lifted its vail, showing to me—the face of my wife! A pale, woeful face, full of anguish, remorse, and fear, yet stronger than all other expressions was one of detestation in the eyes she fixed on me, as she offered me the cup, and vanished with the same weird laugh."

"A singular coincidence I allow, but, my friend, remember she was in your thoughts, and by long brooding over this unhappy matter you had, doubtless, excited yourself more than you knew."

"As you will; hear the sequel, and then decide. A few weeks after this third dream Leonie's conduct roused my jealousy, and, fancying that a rival was the cause of her unhappiness, I resolved to learn the truth. One day when she went out alone I searched her room, and, base, dishonorable as it was, I examined her *secrétaire,* thinking letters might be found. In a secret drawer I found something which alarmed me more than any lover's *billet doux.* A little ebony and silver casket, and in it—" here he bent suddenly and breathed into my ear with a look that haunts me still, the one word—"arsenic!"

It startled me, but I concealed my alarm, and answered, gravely, "You are sure it was like the box in the dream, and that its contents *were* poison?"

"I could swear to it, for it was too peculiar to be mistaken, and the dream too deeply impressed upon my memory to be forgotten. If you doubt my word on the latter point, judge for yourself." And producing a little case from his breast, Monsieur Normande laid a few grains of white powder before me. I tested it, and at once pronounced it arsenic. With a groan he replaced the case, and added, "I had seen her turn in confusion from the *secrétaire,* when I entered suddenly one day, and more than once, as I took my favorite draught from her, I saw that her hand trembled and her eye fell before mine. This discovery suggested the dreadful suspicion that she hated me for separating her from some lover, or that she was possessed by that mysterious malady which often afflicts those who seem most blest. Her manner strengthened the latter belief, for all inquiries failed to confirm my fear of a rival. At times her eyes looked fondly on me, and she seemed longing to confess some hidden pain, or doubt, or tenderness. Then again I would surprise a look so dark, so full of reproach, suspicion and anguish, that my heart stood still within me. She evidently suffers, but suffers in silence, and her health is giving way. She has refused medical advice, but consented to come hither for country air and quiet. Her sudden interest in you, amazed me, but your well-known skill and success made me gladly accede to her wish; and now, that I have told you all, I leave the poor child in your hands. For God's sake do something to restore her, or this dreadful life will kill us both!"

As he paused, and leaned his face upon his hands in an uncontrollable paroxysm of grief, a long silence fell upon the room. I broke it by saying cheerfully, as I rose:

"Let me see madame, and hear her confession, then I can act. Believe me, I fancy it is only some womanish pique or whim, some little trouble which you have magnified, and so made yourselves miserable, as young people often do while learning to live happily together."

"But the poison," he cried with a shudder. "I have my idea about that, and will soon prove its truth. Now let me go; leave this sad tangle in my hands, and compose yourself for whatever the end may be."

He wrung my hand, and without a word led me to madame. At her door he paused, to whisper imploringly:

"Be tender with her, Doctor, remember she is so young, and has been motherless for years."

Reassuring him by a glance, we entered, to find the young lady pacing the room with restless steps, and every sign of feverish impatience. As she paused and watched us approach, I caught, for a single instant, the expression of which her husband spoke. A keen, dark, suspicious look, that made her fair face tragical, and caused me to fear that he was right. Like a flash it vanished, and with a charming smile, she offered her hand, as she welcomed me. As I bowed over it, my eye glanced quickly at the antique ring glittering on the left hand, which played nervously with the ribbons of her *peignoir*. It was too peculiar to be forgotten when once seen, and might well impress one's imagination, even in a dream.

"A thousand pardons for detaining Dr. Velsor so long, but in listening to his interesting travels in Germany, I forgot the flight of time. Now I shall yield him entirely to you, Leonie. Good night, sleep well, *ma amie*."

As he spoke, Normande, who had resumed his cool gentleness of manner, bent, and touched her forehead with his lips, waved his hand to me, as much in warning as adieu, and left the room like one glad to escape. Without a word, madame turned, as if to resume her place in the *fauteuil* beside the fire; but the mirror showed me a face pallid with such mute suffering, that my heart ached for the poor young creature. To put her at ease, and satisfy certain doubts of my own, I talked of her health in a paternal manner, and won from her the frankest replies. She was perfectly well in body, and all her suffering was mental, as I soon satisfied myself. The instant I touched upon that point, she shrunk into herself, and regarded me with a suspicious look, and the hasty question—

"What has Louis told you?"

"Nothing, except that you suffer and will give no reason for your suffering."

"He has no suspicion of the cause then?"

"None, and it afflicts him deeply, that you withhold your confidence from one who loves you so tenderly."

"Loves!" she echoed, with a bitter smile, "yes, he is a model husband, tender, devoted, and patient as an angel. I should be a happy woman, and yet I am utterly miserable."

The words seemed to break from her against her will, for checking the tears that sprung to her eyes, she stretched her hands to me, exclaiming passionately—

"Ah, help me to understand him, to cure him, to make him happy, if that be possible. I love him ardently, and when I married him, I hoped to be all in all to him. But he soon changed, and now there is a barrier between us, that I cannot pass. You deceive yourself, he does *not* love me, he tries to do his duty, but he cannot forget some happier woman."

"I assure, madame, he adores you, and you alone, I know this, for fancying you might have cause for jealousy, with so young and handsome a man, I questioned him, and he rendered it impossible to doubt his love and truth toward you."

I spoke earnestly, feeling sure that my words would heal the breach between the fond and foolish pair; but to my bewilderment, she uttered a cry of despair, and wrung her hands, exclaiming incoherently—

"Then heaven pity me, and help poor Louis! Ah, it is horrible to have my fear confirmed by you. He loves, and yet detests me—he tries to hide the truth from me, but I know it, and my life is ruined."

"What fear, tell me, I entreat you," and I held the hands she was beating distractedly together.

"He is a monomaniac; he loves and loathes me by turns; he is tempted to destroy me, yet cannot nerve his hand to do it, or own the awful truth," she cried.

"Great heavens, what an unhappy mania for self-torture these children possess," I said to myself. "Are both mad? or which is sane! That I must discover at once, or mischief will come of this mysterious mistake."

"Madame, compose yourself, and answer me a few plain questions," I said, authoritatively. "What induces you to think your husband a monomaniac?"

She obeyed like a child, and answered with a sob.

"At first he was all a woman could ask; lover and husband in one, and I was very happy, for I soon learned to love him. Suddenly he changed, grew sad and restless, moody and gay by turns. This increased; he started in his sleep; often walked his room all night; shunned me at times, or watched me with strange scrutiny, as if he feared or suspected something. Then he would relent, be kind and devoted, but never with the former warmth and earnestness. Something burdened and afflicted him, and he would not confide in me. I thought he did not love me, and tried to leave him free from my society, but he haunted me, growing gloomier day by day. Then a dreadful fear possessed me, that he was not himself, for, at times, he frightens me by his violence. As we drove, he suddenly broke a long silence by exclaiming, with a look that made my blood cold—

"'If it *is* true, I could find it in my heart to kill you, with my own hand!' then seeing my terror, he clasped me in his arms, crying passionately—'Leonie, Leonie, forgive me! I am not worthy of you.'"

"This was the cause of your fainting then?"

"Yes, I am not strong, and it startled me. I was myself again in a moment, but it was so sweet to be the object of his care; to feel his arms about me, his kisses on my cheek, that I feigned unconsciousness till you came. Pardon me, for I love him, and we live like strangers now."

Tears streamed through the fingers of the hands she clasped before her face, and for a moment her sobs were the only sound in the room.

"My child, take heart; your fear is groundless, I will prove this to you. But first tell me truly, do you possess a little casket of ebony and silver?"

She started, dropped her hands, and glanced askance at me, as she said slowly, reluctantly—

"Yes, why ask me that?"

"Do you keep it yonder in a secret drawer of that cabinet?" I added, pointing—

"Yes," and the word fell just audibly from lips as white as ashes now.

"And in it there is—arsenic!"

Colorless, and rigid as a statue she sat, staring at me as if I had read her heart. No answer was needed, I saw the truth in her face, and trying to remove her fear, I added, gently—

"Tell me why it is there, and for whom it is to be used. I think I know, so speak freely."

"How do you know this?" she asked in a shrill whisper.

"Your husband told me."

"Louis! impossible!"

"He was jealous, he searched and found it," I began, but starting to her feet, she cried indignantly, yet with a smile at this proof of love—

"Ah, he suspects, he spies upon me, he hunts out my secrets, and believes that I have given him a rival! I thought he was indifferent, I know him better now. Let him search again, and he will find the casket—empty."

Crossing the room, she flung open the *secrétaire;* tore out the drawer, and, with the ebony box in her hand, turned to me, saying with mingled shame and dignity—

"To you I will confess my folly first. He thought me beautiful, and when my secret trouble lessened my bloom, I feared he would find me ugly, and lose the little love he had for me. My maid told me that arsenic gave one the most dazzling complexion, and I used it. I knew it was dangerous, but for his sake, I would have ventured my life. Now you tell me that he loves me, I fling it away, I forgive him everything, and bless you for the comfort you bring me to-night."

With an impulsive gesture, she was about to throw the box into the fire, but I caught her hand, saying, as I put the dangerous toy in my pocket—

"Let me keep it, dear madame, till I can prove to your husband that he has misjudged you. Sit and listen to the truth, for his confession will complete your happiness."

Then in brief, but earnest words, I told all that Normande had confided to me. She listened breathlessly, and when I paused, exclaimed with a sigh, and a smile of mingled joy and pain—

"Ah, how we have tormented ourselves with these secret follies! My vanity and his superstition, have nearly ruined us. But the dream! that was strange. Will he forget it? will he believe my word, and love me in spite of the veiled phantom that wears my shape?"

"I shall banish these fancies by showing him a living, loving woman, who will bring him only health and happiness in her fair hand. Sleep now, my child, and wake to a new life tomorrow," I answered rising.

With the impulsive gesture of a child, she bent her graceful head and pressed a grateful kiss on my withered hand, as she murmured—

"Surely heaven sent you to me. How shall I thank you as I ought?"

Touched, yet anxious to calm her, I answered playfully:

"Sound my praises as a successful healer of heart complaints. Your cure is decidedly a miracle, madame."

She laughed a happy girlish laugh, that well became her fresh lips, and answered with a pretty blush—

"There was much truth in that seeming falsehood, for my heart *did* ache day and night, and but for you, I think it would have broken soon. You'll not tell Louis all my folly?"

"Nay, I leave that for you, well knowing that the time is near when nothing will be so easy and so sweet as the confession of lover's follies."

"Will that time ever come? It sounds too beautiful to be true," and a strangely wistful look saddened the violet eyes, as they gazed full of love and longing on the miniature of her young husband, which she drew from her bosom.

A foreboding thrill passed over me, and a sudden wish to find Normande took possession of me so strongly, that I hastily made my compliments, and left madame standing in the ruddy circle of the fire-light, smiling down on that inanimate face with a tender beauty in her own, which stamped the little picture on my memory forever.

The salon was empty, and the servant whom I summoned was sure his master had retired. Being anxious to tell my good news, I bade him lead me to M. Normande's apartment. No one answered my tap, and half opening the door, I peeped in. He was not there, but a portrait of madame in her bridal dress, caught, and allured my eye. Stepping across the room, I examined it with interest, and the happy consciousness that, thanks to my exertions, the bloom on that painted cheek would soon be out-rivalled by that upon the living one. A little table stood below the picture, holding a silver salver and cup evidently newly filled with Normande's favorite draught.

"Strange contradictions of the human heart," I mused. "He dreads poison, yet daily empties this cup which might so easily bring him death. He fears, and yet he trusts her. Ah, well, love will work a healing miracle for both."

My old eyes filled at the thought, and pulling out my handkerchief, I dried them, as I stood there, looking up at the lovely image before me. As my host was invisible, I left word with his valet that I would see him early in the morning, and departed to bed.

With the impatience of one who longs to finish a good work, I was early astir. As I went towards Normande's apartment, I met his wife in a charming costume, and with a face as fresh and fair as the roses in her hands.

She greeted me warmly, saying, with an enchanting blush and smile—

"I could wait no longer to ask Louis to forgive me, and am trying to gather courage to go in, and wake him with a wifely kiss."

"You have not seen him then?" I said, hoping that the explanation had been made.

"No, I came up last night to tell him all, soon after you left me, but he was not here, and, as I crept away, he passed me with a strange look, and locked himself in;" and she brushed away a tear that lay glittering on her cheek, like the dew upon her flowers.

"I had not seen him either, therefore he had not learned the truth. Go now and call him, dear madame, he cannot refuse to answer such a summons."

Smiling, she glided to the door and tapped. It was not fastened and swung open; she paused a moment on the threshold, then, softly calling his name, she entered. Knowing that I should be *de trop,* I turned away, but had taken only a step or two, when a cry of mortal fear and anguish rung through the house. With the speed of a young man, I dashed into the room, to find madame senseless on her husband's bosom, as he lay dead and cold upon his bed. The cup stood empty on the table, and beside it the ebony casket, half hidden by a paper bearing these words:

"Leonie, adieu; I will torment you no longer. I heard your voice last night, saying that I should be satisfied, for, when next I found the hidden casket, it should be empty. I *have* found it, for you dropped it as you stole away, before your work was done. I *am* satisfied, and knowing whose hand would have drugged my cup, I add the poison, and drink the draught, preferring death to the misery of life without your love."

As I read it, a great terror fell upon me, for it was *I* who had murdered him. I saw in a flash how the fatal box came there, and what construction he had put upon its presence. In drawing out my handkerchief, the box had fallen noiselessly on the velvet carpet, and I had not missed it. Seeing Leonie stealing away, remembering the broken words which had reached him as she

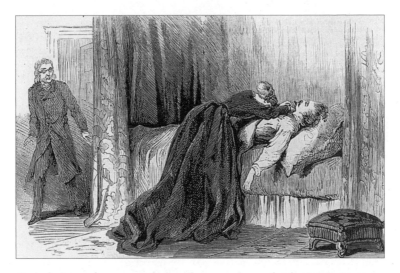

"I dashed into the room, to find madame senseless on her husband's bosom, as he lay dead and cold upon his bed."

raised her voice, and finding the poison in his room, the old suspicion was terribly confirmed, and in a paroxysm of despair, the unhappy young man destroyed himself, believing his wife mad or false.

I could have torn my grey hair in remorseful grief, for this tragical end to my work. If he had only seen *me*, instead of her, what a different hour that would have been! I went to carry blissful tidings, which would have brightened life, and by a most accursed chance, I left a terrible suspicion which tempted him to death!

He was past help, and all my care was needed for the poor young widow. The awful shock, the sudden fall from the highest joy to the deepest woe, killed her, and the words she uttered the night before, were a prophecy, for she did die of a broken heart. I stayed with her to the end, and when I had seen the young pair laid to their rest, I sorrowfully went my way, comforting myself with the hope that they were happily reunited in a world, where human frailties and follies could never sadden nor separate the hearts that "loved not wisely but too well."

Fate in a Fan

"YOU HAVE YOUR WEAPON, LEONTINE?"

"Yes."

"Use it well to-night, for this person must be finished at once."

"You will show no mercy?"

"None! I hate him, and nothing but his ruin will satisfy me. Remember that."

"I dare not forget."

The low voices ceased, as if the speakers had passed on, and a moment afterward a young man glided noiselessly down the corridor, vanishing in a side-passage which led to the main entrance. His face wore a startled look; his keen eyes shone, and his nervous hand closed like a vice, as he muttered, grimly:

"Weapon! hate! ruin! I knew there was deviltry afloat; to-night I've found a clue, and will follow it up to the death."

A tall, strikingly handsome man, in the brilliant uniform of an Austrian officer, stood in the hall, evidently waiting for some one, as he idly pulled a rose to pieces, humming the refrain of an Italian love-song.

"You disappear and appear like a spirit. Where have you been, Rolande?" he asked, in a gay tone, as the new-comer's touch on his shoulder disturbed his reverie.

"Finding that your *tête-à-tête* with madame's pretty *soubrette* was likely to be prolonged, I strolled away and lost myself among the passages of the hotel. Must you play again to-night, Ulf?"

"I must, or else how recover my losses? I fear to think of them, and see no salvation but in some turn of luck."

The handsome face darkened for a moment, as the Austrian flung away the relics of the rose, and set his heel on them with a petulant gesture.

"This infatuation costs you dear. How will it end, my poor friend?"

"The devil, patron of gamesters, only knows. It can scarcely be worse than it is, and may be better. I cling to that hope, and play on."

"You would not listen to my warnings," began Rolande; but the other broke in:

"I hate presentiments, and would take no warning, even from you, Alcide. Let me go my own way. I cannot in honor stop now. St. Pierre must have his revenge at any cost."

"No fear of that," muttered Rolande, adding, in a lower tone: "One word, and I am dumb. If I can convince you that you have not had fair play, will you quit this dangerous place?"

The young officer opened his blue eyes wide, pulled his blonde mustache thoughtfully for a moment, and knit his brows, as if perplexed. Then his face cleared, and breaking into a boyish laugh, he clapped his friend on the shoulder, saying, blithely:

"You croaking raven! you infected me with your doubts for an instant; but I scorn to harbor them. I'll not let you play the spy for me; nor will I be convinced by any but the most honorable proofs."

"Good! I am satisfied. Come on, we are late, and the old one does not like to wait."

"Ah, you go now with alacrity, though usually I cannot get you up without much coaxing. You are a sphinx to me, Alcide."

"I'll solve my riddles for you soon. *En avant!*" cried Rolande, mounting the stairs, and leading the way to an apartment on the first floor.

If the little tableau which greeted them had been prepared, it certainly had been done with skill, and was very effective. A white-haired, soldierly old man sat in an antique chair placed beside a small green-covered table, and leaning over him, in an attitude of enchanting grace, was his daughter—a slender little creature, shrouded in black lace, with no ornament but tube roses in the bosom. Not beautiful, for the face was pale and thin, the lips almost colorless, and the figure so slight, that even the profuse falls of rich lace could not entirely conceal it. Eyes of wonderful depth and brilliancy, and luxuriant hair of the purest gold, were her only charms, except the grace which marked every gesture, and a voice of peculiar sweetness.

M. St. Pierre's patrician face reminded one of the Frenchmen of the old school—the gallant, pleasure-loving gentlemen, who flashed out their swords at the first breath of insult, who served king or mistress with equal devotion, and rode gayly to the guillotine, with a nosegay at the breast, a laugh on the lips. Whatever his vices, they were concealed under the most perfect manners; and if his life held any secret sin or shame, no trace of it ever appeared in his aristocratic old face, which seldom varied its expression of serene suavity.

As the young men approached, mademoiselle turned to meet them with a shy smile, and her father waved his hand, exclaiming, cordially:

"Ah, I have to thank you for remembering the old man, and sacrificing an hour to give him his one pleasure."

Bergamo, the Austrian, and Rolande, the Frenchman, paid their compliments in nearly the same words, and mademoiselle received them with the same courtesy, yet some indescribable shade of difference was perceptible in her manner. Bergamo kissed her hand, with undisguised devotion; Rolande merely bowed, but the kiss brought no color to her cheek, while the colder salutation made her brilliant eyes fall, the sensitive lips tremble for a second, and though she answered the Austrian's gay flattery with badinage as gay, she evidently listened intently to her countryman's chat with her father.

"Can we not tempt you, M. Rolande?" said the old man, hospitably, when at length they seated themselves about the table.

"Monsieur forgets that I know nothing of the game, and have no gold to lose."

Something in the sharp, cold tone of the young man's voice made St. Pierre cast a quick glance at him. But the dark, grave face was impenetrable, and setting down the sharpness to some natural twinge of shame, at confessing ignorance and poverty, the elder man returned to his cards, and left his guest to amuse himself as he might.

This did not appear a difficult matter, for, as if possessed by some new whim, Rolande seated himself beside mademoiselle, and began to talk. She was evidently well trained, for no sign of emotion was now visible, and the dangerous eyes met his own freely, as she conversed with skill and spirit.

Bergamo, meanwhile, played with the reckless daring of a desperate man, and, as usual, began by winning just enough to whet his appetite and lure him on to large ventures. He fixed his whole mind upon the game, and did not allow his attention to be distracted by the timely chat going on behind him. St. Pierre played with the composure of an accomplished gamester, losing tranquilly, yet expressing naive surprise at his ill luck. Once or twice he glanced at his daughter, as if Rolande's sudden interest amused him, and when the players paused a moment, at the close of the first game, he said, with a persuasive smile: "Rolande, give us a little music, I beseech you. It disturbs no one, but refreshes all, and you, Leontine, rest, my child; you are too pale to-night."

Both obeyed; mademoiselle leaned back in her chair, and the young man seated himself at the instrument, glad of a moment to collect his thoughts. While he talked, he had watched the girl closely, but discovered nothing to aid him in his search. Now as he played, he continued to watch, yet gained little light on the puzzle which perplexed him. Leontine merely drew out her fan, and languidly observed the game, while listening to the delicious music that filled the room. She sat where she could see Bergamo's cards, yet seemed not to avail herself of the fact, though now and then she gave a smiling reply to his questions.

"Is treachery the weapon?" thought Rolande, playing softly, with his eyes in the mirror, which permitted him to see the group without turning. "No, she makes no signals; St. Pierre never looks at her, she never speaks to him. Her eyes do the mischief. Ulf grows excited now, plays carelessly, and turns often to address her. Poor lad, they will beguile him to his ruin!"

The entrance of a servant with wine and coffee brought a new suspicion to the jealous observer, for Leontine rose at once, dismissed the man, and preparing a cup with care, brought it to Bergamo, herself.

"Ah, is that it? Will she drug him slightly, and let the old villain fleece him before my eyes?" cried Rolande to himself, pausing with a discord.

The Austrian was lifting the fragrant draught to his lips, when his friend's hand arrested him.

"No, Ulf, you must drink nothing to-night; you are not well, and I am to watch over you. Pardon, mademoiselle; do not tempt him."

Rolande's tone was perfectly natural, but Bergamo caught the warning conveyed, and submitted with a good-humored laugh.

"As you will; I regret the loss of nectar brewed by such fair hands; but being under orders, I must obey."

"May he not drink wine?" asked Leontine, following Rolande as he carried the cup away.

"His physician forbids anything after dinner; he is forgetful, but I love my friend, and watch over him with *vigilance.*"

As he slightly emphasized the last word, Rolande glanced at the girl, who averted her eyes, with a peculiar smile. Bent on satisfying his suspicion, the young man added, with the cup still in his hand:

"Will mademoiselle permit me to enjoy the draught so kindly prepared for another."

She bowed carelessly, and the slender hand, that was lifting a glass, never trembled, as Rolande sipped the coffee, with his keen eyes on her face.

"Wrong again," he thought, as she went to carry the wine to her father; "perhaps I have deceived myself; and yet those words, my own forebodings, and the mystery which surrounds the St. Pierres! What weapon *could* the old man have meant?"

As he stood musing, a light object on the dark carpet at his feet caught his attention; absently taking it up, he saw that it was a white lace fan, with a pearl and golden handle, a dainty toy for a fair hand. Before he had time to examine it further, Leontine returned, and the instant she saw it, a curious expression of annoyance came into her face. A careless observer would not have seen it, but Rolande was on the watch, and caught the slight frown at once.

"Thanks, it is mine," she said, extending her hand to reclaim it.

"Pardon, permit me to admire it a moment. I have no sisters, and these coquettish trifles are charming mysteries to me," replied Rolande, with a gallant air, as he unfurled the delicate fan and moved it gently to and fro, affecting to examine it, while he covertly took note of her nervous little laugh, and the faint color which came into her pale cheeks.

His quick eye ran over the fan, hoping to find there some sign of foul play, for he had heard of the Spanish women, who enact both tragedies and comedies with the expressive by-play of their fans. No cabalistic figures anywhere appeared among the light wreaths upon the lace, no mirrors on the pearl framework, no concealed stiletto in the golden handle, to which he gave a shy twist, while praising the filigree which covered it.

"Baffled a third time," muttered Rolande to himself, when he could no longer retain the fan without rudeness, for Leontine stood silently waiting beside him. Just as her fingers closed over it, he saw something which made him regret so soon relinquishing it. As she waited, Leontine had unconsciously laid one hand on the tall coffee-urn, and had not removed it till he gave up the fan, though several of the delicate finger-tips were blistered by the hot silver.

"Nothing but some intense anxiety could have made her forgetful of pain like that. There is some secret about that toy, and I have missed it. I must get back the fan and discover it. First, let me see again how she uses it."

As those thoughts swept through his mind, St. Pierre called to his daughter:

"Leontine, a lump of sugar in my wine." Bland as the voice was, and paternal the smile which accompanied the slight request, the girl started, caught up the crystal basin and glided away, holding the fan tightly in one hand.

Rolande strolled to the window-recess and soon seemed absorbed in the evening papers. Leontine resumed her place by Bergamo, and the game went on. By furtive glances Rolande discovered three things which confirmed his suspicions that all was not right. The Austrian played badly, seeming to have lost his usual skill strangely; he grew pale and silent, his brilliant eyes looked dull and heavy, and the little that he said was neither gay nor sensible. The second discovery was that Leontine fanned herself incessantly, but seemed to take no interest in the game, though her father often addressed some tender remark to her as he played with unusual care. The third was, that the scent of tube roses filled the air, for the spring night was sultry, and a great vase of them stood near the girl.

"Is he drunk with love, overpowered with despair, or oppressed with this heavy perfume?" thought Rolande, eyeing his friend with anxiety and wonder. Rapidly he recalled all the facts concerning their acquaintance with the St. Pierres. The old man had been taken ill in the Tuileries Gardens, the friends had helped him home, seen the daughter, and called the next day to inquire for the father. Rolande had been struck with the loveliness of the girl, who naively owned that she was a stranger in Paris, and devoted herself to her invalid father, who could not bear much society. The lovely eyes, wet with tears, touched the heart of susceptible Bergamo, and finding that his society was agreeable to Monsieur St. Pierre, he fell into the way of frequenting the quiet *salon* to play with the father and admire the daughter. Rolande felt little interest in them, but for his friend's sake made inquiries about them, found that they were unknown except to a few young men, who, attracted by mademoiselle, had lost heavily at play to monsieur. Bergamo's fine fortune was already nearly squandered by the recklessly generous young man, and Rolande, whom poverty had made prudent, tried to restrain him from gambling, his besetting sin. Large sums had St. Pierre won from him, but was not yet satisfied, and the calm looker-on felt that some hidden motive increased the old man's natural rapacity. Alcide set himself to discover this motive, for in spite of St. Pierre's polished manners and perpetual benignity, the acute young man distrusted him from the first. Leontine was evidently a puppet in her father's hands; but, though she obediently smiled on Bergamo, she unconsciously betrayed that she loved his friend. Alcide saw this, and pitied her; but having no heart to give, he tried by cool indifference to quench her timid hopes.

He was roused from his reverie by an exclamation from Ulf, who struck the table with a feeble laugh as he threw down a card, saying, "Another hand like that, and I am finished!"

"You joke, *mon ami;* your princely fortune will sustain the loss of many trifling draughts like mine," replied St. Pierre, dealing with his severest smile and a transient glitter of exultation in his hard eye.

"You play badly; I fancy the odor of these flowers oppresses you; allow me to remove them, mademoiselle, for you also look as if they were too powerful for you."

Rolande placed the great rose on a distant table, and returning, leaned on his friend's chair, troubled and perplexed by the pallor of the girl's face, the strange indifference of Bergamo, and the expression of St. Pierre's inscrutable countenance. Leontine rose at once, saying, with a wan smile:

"I live on odors, but regret my forgetfulness of others;" and casting a glance at her father, she passed into an inner room. Rolande followed her, unobserved, for the old man was intent on the last hand of the game. An uncontrollable impulse led the young man to that inner room, and he lifted the curtain which separated it from the *salon* just in time to see the girl drop her fan, tear the flowers from her bosom, and lean far out at the open window, gasping for air. With a noiseless stride, Alcide clutched the fan before he spoke.

"Mademoiselle is ill; let me call her maid, or bring wine," he said, softly.

She sprang up with a startled look, saw the fan in his hand, and tried to speak, but her white lips made no sound, though her hands were outstretched imploringly.

"No, you are too much overcome; permit me to help you;" and placing her on the couch with gentle force, Rolande moved the fan over her, unmindful of the nervous grasp she laid on his arm.

"One moment; give it back for a moment, I entreat you!" she whispered, eagerly.

"Not till I discover the secret which it holds," he answered, in a low, stern tone.

With a long sigh Leontine's head fell back, and she fainted, looking like one who gave herself up for lost. Shocked, but not turned from his purpose, Alcide sprinkled water on her face, and fanned assiduously, with his eyes fixed on the fragile weapon the strange girl had evidently feared to give up. A strong perfume filled the air, yet no flowers were in the room, for Leontine had flung the tube roses from her bosom into the street—a subtle, penetrating perfume, which made the temples throb after inhaling a few breaths of it, and speedily produced a delicious drowsiness. Rolande lifted the fan to his nostrils and satisfied himself that the fragrance came from it. No aperture was visible, and, impatient at being foiled so long, he struck the handle sharply on a marble console near; the pearl under the filigree was shattered by the blow, and disclosed a slender crystal vial, with a spring stopper, which a touch on some unsuspected ornament would lift. Shutting and pocketing this tiny traitor, Rolande pried into the delicate structure of the fan, discovering that the golden sticks were hollow, and that the hateful perfume rising through them was effectually diffused with every waft of the fan. He was still examining this artful toy when Leontine recovered, saw that her secret was known, and clasping her hands, she whispered, in a tone of despair:

"I will confess all, but oh, save me from my father!"

"Your father!" ejaculated the young man, in astonishment.

"Yes, I dread him more than death. Hush, can he not hear us?" she said, trying to rise, as if to assure herself that no one was listening. Rolande stole to the entrance, peeped beyond the curtain, saw that St. Pierre was absorbed in play, and returned, saying, in a reassuring tone:

"Confide in me, my poor child; I will defend you if you give me all the truth."

"Ah, it is bitter to confess such dishonor, and to *you,*" she murmured, hiding her face.

"Regard me as your friend, for I swear to you I will do my best to shield you, if I can also save Ulf," cried Rolande, sitting beside her, and gently taking her thin hand in his.

"So kind! God will reward you, and I shall not long burden any one. The poison is killing me by inches, but I dared not rebel," she answered, glancing at the broken fan with a shudder.

"Speak quickly! is it as I suspect?"

"Yes, that subtle Indian perfume intoxicates and stupefies whoever breathes it. My father learned the secret of it when a soldier in the East. He had the fan made as if for a harmless odor, and forced me to use it with that horrible stuff hidden in it. I sit by his opponents when he plays, and while they fancy it is love, or wine, or the heavily-scented flowers I wear, which excites and bewilders them, my treacherous fan dulls their senses, and my father plunders them."

The poor pale face turned scarlet with shame, as the last words left her lips, and she wrung her hands, as if a proud spirit rebelled against dishonor.

"Ah, and this, then, is the cause of Ulf's strange headaches lately, his watchfulness and alternate lethargy and excitement. Leontine, would you have killed him with this accursed spell?" demanded Rolande.

"No, oh, no! that I could never do. My father hates his family for some old slight or insult, and desires to ruin him, nothing more. It is myself whom I kill," she added, in a broken voice.

"Yourself! how? why? tell me all, I conjure, my poor girl."

"Do you think I can breathe for months, unharmed, a perfume which affects the magnificent health of your friend in a week or two? It is killing me slowly, but surely, and I dare not escape."

"Your father permits this?" cried Rolande, indignantly.

"He is proud and poor; he loves ease and pleasure; I can help to earn them for him; I obey my poor mother's last command, and cling to him through everything."

"There shall be an end to this, and St. Pierre shall restore what he has unfairly won, or be given up to the law," said Rolande, in a tone of decision, which proved to Leontine that the old man would receive no mercy at his hands. She turned her wan face toward him, saying, beseechingly:

"Let *me* suffer, for life is valueless to me, but he finds happiness in it; leave him to enjoy it and repent, if he can."

"Have you always led a life like this?" asked the young man, touched by the misery in her melancholy eyes.

"No; I remember a time when I was happy, but misfortune came, my mother died, and I had no one to cling to but my father."

"Could you not break away, and find friends elsewhere?"

"I tried that lately, but he forbid it; he was very cruel, and threatened to betray my secret," sobbed the girl.

"What secret?"

"I will never tell it!" her lips said, with a passionate resolve; but her eyes told it eloquently, as they sank before Alcide's.

His dark face softened, as he laid his hand on her bowed head, and the tenderest pity lent its music to his voice, as he said, in the friendliest tone:

"Will you put yourself under my old mother's care for a time? She will welcome and befriend you, and so will the little wife whom I am to bring home in a month."

"You are kind, but I have another friend who will take me in when my father deserts me. Think no more of me, but save Bergamo, and deal as kindly as you can with the old man. Hark! they are rising! Go at once; adieu, adieu!"

She caught his hand, kissed it with pathetic humility, and waved him from her with a gesture of farewell. He went just in time to see Ulf drop his head on the table with a groan, as St. Pierre handed him an account of the sums lately lost, saying, with an evil smile:

"It is, of course, unnecessary for me to remind my friend that debts of honor should be promptly paid."

Bergamo sprang up, haggard and desperate, exclaiming, hotly:

"Rest satisfied; you shall be paid to the last franc, though it leaves me a beggar."

"Give yourself no uneasiness, Ulf; *I* shall settle this account;" and Rolande came between them, calm and stern as fate.

"Is it permitted to inquire with what M. Rolande will discharge this trifling sum?" asked St. Pierre, as he pointed to the heavy sum total set down upon the paper, and laughed a soft, sneering laugh.

"With this!" and Alcide displayed the shattered fan.

Bergamo stared wonderingly at it, but St. Pierre's extended hand fell suddenly, and a flash of wrath glittered in his eyes. Only for a moment. He was a consummate actor, and the false smile, the bland tone, the grand air had become second nature. With a slight shrug, he said, quietly:

"Pardon, if I fail to perceive the point of the reply; a woman's bauble cannot pay a man's debts."

"A woman's bauble helped to win that money, and, being fraudulently gained, you will not receive a sou of it, but will restore that already secured, or this frail toy goes to tell its secret to the Préfet of the Police," returned Rolande, with an ominous gesture, as he showed the empty handle.

"Ah, the little traitress betrays her father to her lover, it seems! She has more courage than I thought, and will need it all. You win the game, *mon ami,* and I admire your address; but before I restore the sums you mention, I have a desire to know what is to follow that unusual proceeding?"

St. Pierre had turned white to the lips, and his eyes fell for an instant, and then he was himself again, ready for anything, and wearing the air of a man whom dishonor could not touch or danger daunt.

"For your daughter's sake, I will be silent, if you restore your ill-gotten gains and leave Paris at once. You agree to this, Ulf?" asked Rolande, trying to rouse his friend, who looked from one to the other, as if bewildered.

"Yes, anything, Alcide; I leave it all to you," he said, hastily.

"Good! Then, monsieur, you know my demand and its alternative. Allow me to quote your own words, and remind you that 'debts of honor should be promptly paid.'"

The young man's look and words stung St. Pierre like a blow; but he merely smiled the evil smile, and extended his shapely white hand with a motion which was a menace, as he said, slowly, pointing toward the inner room:

"Has my charming daughter informed her lover of one little fact which may affect his passion? Merely that her mother was not my wife?"

"That fact cannot affect me, except to increase my pity, for I am not the poor girl's lover, but affianced to another. To me the sins of her father far outweigh the misfortunes of her mother," returned Rolande, unmoved.

"I play a losing game and miss my last card; so be it, I am an old soldier. Leontine, my little darling, bring hither the roll of notes from my *secrétaire.*"

As he called, in a tone of mocking tenderness, the curtains parted, and his daughter appeared, looking like a ghost risen from its grave at the summons of a master whom it dared not disobey. An awful change had passed over her since Rolande left her, for life, strength, and color seemed gone, and she moved with a feeble gait, extended hands and vacant eyes, like one groping the way through utter darkness. One pale hand held the notes, the other, the tiny vial from the fan, which had slipped, unobserved, from Alcide's pocket as he bent over her.

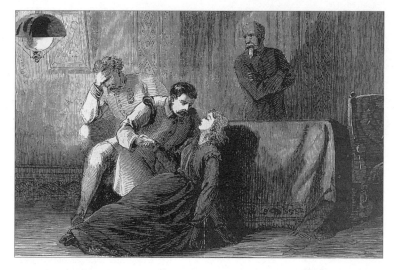

"In the act of speaking, her lips grew still, as the poor girl's blighted life ended."

"Here, father, forgive me, and quit this evil life, as I do. Alcide, take back this proof of my treachery; you may need it; I have left enough."

"It is half gone, the powerful attar! what have you done, poor child?" cried Rolande, supporting her as she would have fallen at his feet.

"I drank it; one drop taken will kill quickly, and there was no other way. Forget me, and be happy with the little wife."

In the act of speaking, her lips grew still, as with one look of hopeless love the poor girl's blighted life ended, and she lay at rest on the only heart that could have redeemed for her the erring past. Bergamo covered up his face, but St. Pierre stood like a man of stone, giving no sign of grief, except the ghostly pallor of his face, and the great drops that shone upon his forehead.

As Rolande reverently kissed those pale lips, and laid the lifeless figure tenderly down, the old man flung the money at his
feet, and with a superb gesture of defiance and dismissal, moved
them from his presence. They went without a word; but, glancing back, saw him bow his white head and gather his dead
daughter in his arms, as if he clung despairingly to the frail
faithful creature whom he had killed.

Which Wins?

I TELL YOU, DELMAR, it will be as I say. The Viennese Thyra will marry the rich Spaniard, and the Polish Nadine will accept the charming villa at Vichy, and the two hundred thousand francs which the old marquis offers to settle upon her."

"We shall see. It is evident that they are rivals, and cordially hate one another, for it is a race between the two beauties to see which will make the best match. Thyra is the handsomest, without doubt, but Nadine is by far the most bewitching and the most dangerous. I'll wager you any amount you like that she will win."

"Done! I say the blonde Viennese will distance the brunette Pole in spite of her *finesse,* for beauty carries the day in nine cases out of ten. By the way, have you any faith in the stories which begin to be whispered about the Spaniard?"

"No. He roused the ill-will of St. Maur at play, and the latter revenges himself by hinting that the count is an adventurer. He may be, for all I know or care, but the fair Thyra had better make her game without delay if she wishes to become a countess."

"It would be friendly to give her a hint of these reports," said Albany, the young Englishman, to his friend.

"Quite unnecessary. These gay butterflies know how to take care of their own interests with a worldly wisdom which amazes me. Thyra hears all the gossip, for her dear friends would not neglect to tell her anything detrimental to her lover. Say nothing, but stand aside and watch the play; it is almost as interesting as roulette."

"If this Thyra had more life she would be altogether divine, but one cannot fall in love with a statue, however handsome. I should like to see her roused, if it were possible," said Albany, yawning.

"Wait a little, and you will have your wish, if I am not mistaken. Nadine has the temper of a little demon, and will not be outdone without a spirited battle. She will rouse your statue for you if she finds her in the way. Let us go and take an observation of the pretty creatures." And taking his friend's arm, Delmar strolled away.

The persons of whom the young men spoke were two of the fine, charming girls who had exchanged their humble homes for the position of waiters upon the guests at the great "Restauration de Dreher," at the Exposition. Three of these girls had already found, not only admirers but husbands, men of wealth and standing. The fair Hungarian had gained the heart of a gentleman from the Faubourg St. Germain, and had just started on her wedding tour. The pretty Tyrolese married an American nabob, and the stately Belgian had returned to her native city the wife of a rich merchant. But, strange as it seemed, the two loveliest of the five still remained unwon, for, spoilt by adulation, they had grown ambitious, and rejected with scorn offers which their companions accepted gratefully. The spirit of rivalry possessed them, and each was so fearful that the other would outstrip her in the race, that both hesitated long in deciding to which of their many suitors they should give the preference. The spirit which animated these charming girls was not without its effect upon their admirers, who, while they laughed at the ladies' little wiles, caprices and spites, yet watched one another sharply, and contended for the prizes more from emulation than love.

As Delmar, the Frenchman, had said, Thyra was the handsomest, being a stately blonde with magnificent hair, sleepy blue eyes, and the figure of a Juno. She was neither very witty nor wise, but her slow smile was pronounced "divine." The movements of her white arms rendered speech unnecessary, and she had sufficient sense to make the most of her charms, and hold her own against the dashing Pole.

Nadine was a brilliant brunette, with eyes like diamonds, vivid red lips, a slender figure, and a foot that won her more compliments than her witty tongue. She possessed that natural grace which is often more attractive than beauty, and a face so arch, piquant, and bewitching, that few could resist its charm. In her national costume, smiling or frowning with capricious coquetry as she tripped to and fro, affecting to be absorbed in her duties and quite unconscious of the admiring glances which followed the little scarlet boots and vivacious face under the blue and silver cap, she was one of the most striking figures in the great *café*.

As the two young men passed on, a slight female figure, wrapped in a large mantle, slipped out of the flowery recess behind them, and vanished with a stifled laugh into another path.

The *café* was comparatively quiet just then, for all the world was at the Palace of Industry, at the grand distribution of prizes by the emperor. Thyra was reposing after her fatigues, and permitting several of her admirers to amuse her, for she already assumed the airs of a *grande dame*. Not far off Nadine was tormenting the old marquis by affecting sudden coldness and disdain.

"Ah, mademoiselle, if you knew the secret I have just learned you would vouchsafe me a smile," murmured the enamored gentleman, putting down his glass with a sigh.

A careless shrug was all the reply he got for this artful remark.

"Heart of ice! She no longer cares if that big Viennese eclipses her; she yields the palm to the lazy one, and owns herself defeated. I fancied my beautiful Nadine possessed too much pride and spirit for that. Her courage made her beauty all-powerful, but, vanquished, she will no longer charm."

"Will monsieur take another bottle?" coolly inquired the girl, with a demure air, as the old gentleman made a feint of rising.

"If mademoiselle will share it with me, for truly I need some consolation," he returned, reseating himself, well pleased.

Filling a couple of glasses, Nadine fixed her brilliant eyes on him, and answered with a significant smile and a gesture full of coquetry, "I drink to the winners."

"My faith, you do not retreat, then?" cried the marquis, tossing off his champagne with enthusiasm.

"Never!" replied Nadine, clinching her rosy hand, with a flash of the black eyes, that caused the marquis to exult in the success of his words:

"See, then, my angel, the matter is easy; for, armed with my little secret, you may annoy, perhaps defeat the amiable plots of the blondine yonder."

"What is this so important a secret? Tell it, and leave me in peace!" exclaimed Nadine, petulantly.

"It has its price," began the marquis.

"*Chut!* then I will not hear it."

"Little miser! I only ask one kiss of that dimpled hand, one smile of those lips, one friendly glance from the eyes that make my day or night."

"Is it about Thyra?" asked the girl, laughing at the sentimental tone of her ancient lover.

"Yes. And she will be ready to annihilate me when she knows that I have betrayed her."

"How did you discover it?"

"By accident. I felt that she hated thee. I suspected some mystery. I watched, and a judiciously-bestowed napoleon gave me the secret in time to prevent thy downfall at the *bal-masqué,* which I hope to give thee soon."

"Tell me—tell me at once!" cried Nadine, eagerly, for his hints alarmed her.

"You agree, then, to the little bargain?"

"Yes, yes, anything; but first the secret," replied the girl, folding her arms, and placing herself beyond his reach.

"Know, then, that Thyra intends to outshine thee in a dress of great magnificence. She affects to confide in thee, to ask thy advice and admire thy taste, but it is merely to learn thy plans and blind thee to her own."

"She is not going in the costume of La Belle Hélène, then?" asked Nadine, knitting her brows with a menacing frown.

"No, she will appear as a marquise of the time of the *grande monarque.*"

"Ah, the traitress! she knows that you will wear a dress of that period, and she insults me by assuming one like it. Good! Two can play at that little game, and, thanks to you, I shall *not* be eclipsed by that false creature." And Nadine's *méchante* face brightened with malicious merriment.

"I have done well, then, and earned my reward?" murmured the marquis.

"Yes, receive it," was her smiling reply, as she surrendered her hand to him. "Hold, it is enough; tell me more, foolish man, and help me to defeat my enemy," she added, the next minute withdrawing it, red with the ardent pressure he had given it.

"Here is the name of the *modiste* who will prepare the costume; I discovered and preserved it for thee. Order what thou wilt, my little angel, in my name, and outshine this Thyra, or I never will forgive thee."

Nadine's eyes sparkled as they rested on her unconscious rival, and her quick wit suggested a way to return treachery for treachery; but she sighed a quick sigh as the marquis made his offer, for she knew what it meant. She did not love him, but his admiration exalted her in the eyes of others; his lavish gifts enhanced her beauty, his assistance would enable her to defeat Thyra's malice, his protection would lift her above want at once, and his name would ennoble her forever, *if* she could win it. He had never offered it as yet, but as she recalled the words and wager of Albany and Delmar she resolved to delay no longer, but "make her game" at once and throw out her rival's afterward. As these thoughts passed through her mind her vivacious face grew grave and pale, and another heavy sigh escaped her.

"My child, what afflicts you?" cried the marquis, alarmed at the sudden change. "Does my offer offend?"

"No, I thank you; yet I do not accept," returned Nadine, with well-feigned regret.

"And why? What means this sudden coldness? Does not Thyra receive the count's gifts freely?"

"She may, for he loves her."

"Great heavens! and do not I adore thee?"

"Not as he adores Thyra."

"Prove it!" cried the marquis, hotly.

"He gives her all she asks," began the girl, pensively.

"Will I not joyfully give thee anything in the world?"

"I think not."

"Try me!"

But Nadine turned timid all at once, dropped her eyes, blushed, and smiled as she picked his bouquet to pieces with the most captivating little air of embarrassment imaginable.

"Nadine, what will the count give Thyra that I will not give thee?" asked the marquis, tenderly.

"His hand and name," answered the girl, with her softest glance.

"Ah, the devil!" cried her lover, drawing back with a start. "Has he already done this?" he asked, anxiously, after a pause.

"Yes." And Nadine told the lie without hesitation, for on it depended her own fate.

"Then, by all the saints, I will not be outdone by him!" exclaimed the marquis, with the reckless ardor of a young man.

"Wilt thou come to Vichy as my wife, Nadine?" he said, slowly, but with the air of one who had decided.

Then, turning her lovely face, radiant with smiles, upon him, she whispered softly, as she put her hand in his caressingly: "I will make thee very happy there, Gustave."

A WEEK LATER, on the morning of the day which was to end in the *bal-masqué* given by the gallant old gentlemen in honor of the fair friends, the two girls met in the room set apart for them at the *café*. Both wore an expression of repressed excitement, and both looked unusually gay and blooming. Thyra was remarkably animated, and Nadine's face shone with some secret satisfaction which she could not conceal.

"You are late, my friend," graciously observed Thyra, smoothing her blonde tresses with a plump, white hand.

"I come at my pleasure. They value me too much to complain," replied Nadine, adjusting her dress with the coquettish care of a pretty woman.

"My poor child, you presume upon your charms, but I warn you it is unwise, for these people soon tire of us, and then it fares ill with us unless we have provided for ourselves," said Thyra, in a superior tone.

"Thanks for the advice. I do not trouble myself about the future. I am as yet too young to fear neglect," replied Nadine, with significant emphasis on the word *young,* for her rival was three years her senior, a fact of which she never neglected to remind her.

"Bah! you are too vain, but I pardon it, and when I am madame la comtesse I will not forget you, little one."

Nadine laughed at the superb air of patronage assumed by her friend, and retorted, blandly, "You will then visit me at Vichy? How kind, how condescending."

"You forget that it will be impossible for one of my rank to visit you there. I say nothing of the arrangement, but it will not be *en règle* for me to visit you," said Thyra, with exasperating politeness.

Still Nadine laughed, and slowly pulled off her gloves, as she replied:

"Ah, I had forgotten that a comtesse with a newly-bought title may not, with propriety, visit the wife of a marquis allied to some of the noblest families in France."

"The wife!" echoed Thyra, with a sneer. "You flatter yourself, then, that this old man will marry you? What folly."

"It may be folly to mate my youth with his age, but he is

fond and generous, and will soon leave me free to enjoy all that he so gladly lavishes upon me."

"A hundred thousand francs, and dishonor. *Mon Dieu,* I do not envy you," cried Thyra, scornfully.

"He will leave me his whole fortune, his rank and his name; I ask no more."

Thyra laughed shrilly, for something in her rival's imperturbable air annoyed her more than her words.

"When I see proofs of the truth of this absurd story, I will believe it."

"See and believe, then," and Nadine lifted her newly-ungloved left hand with a gesture of triumph, for on the third slender finger shone a wedding ring, guarded by a magnificent diamond *solitaire.*

"Married!" cried Thyra, turning pale with envy and chagrin.

"Married, mademoiselle; but I do not ask your compliments yet, for the fact is not to be made known till this evening. It was my whim to serve here one day longer, a marquise in disguise, and Gustave permits me to have my own way in all things."

There was both gall and wormwood in this speech, for it reminded the hearer that her mock marquise would be entirely eclipsed by the real one, and that her count would *not* permit her to have her own way if she married him, as he was both jealous and tyrannical. For a moment she was speechless with anger and mortification, but she recovered herself with an effort, and forcing a smile, swept a stately curtsey, and saying in a tone of ironical deference:

"I congratulate you, madame, upon your success, and wish you a speedy release from monsieur le marquis."

"Thanks, mademoiselle; I heartily return the compliment,

for if you *should* marry the count, I fear you will never live to enjoy your freedom after his death. *Au revoir,* then; we shall meet this evening. I trust your costume is prepared?"

"Quite; and yours?"

"It is ready," and Nadine tripped away with a wicked smile on her lips, leaving her rival to console herself with thoughts of the evening triumph she hoped to win.

So anxious was Thyra to vent her pique, that she arrived at the hotel of the marquis before Nadine, thus losing the satisfaction of making her *entrée* in the presence of her rival. Her costume was charming, for the antique blue and silver brocade set off her fine figure, and the powder in her hair enhanced the bloom of her dazzling complexion. Compliments were profuse, and her spirits rose, for the count was more devoted than ever, and nearer to uttering the long-desired words, she thought.

Just when every one was wondering at her absence, Nadine appeared, and one glance at her assured Thyra that her own reign was over, for the tables had been turned with a vengeance. Nadine wore the costume of a Spanish lady of rank, and wore it with a grace which made it doubly effective. Composed of scarlet, black and gold, the costume was wonderfully becoming, for the rich lace mantilla draped, without concealing, the little figure and lovely face; the little feet were ravishing in slippers which few beside a true Spaniard could have worn, and diamonds as brilliant as her eyes flashed in her dark hair, and shone on wrist and bosom, convincing Thyra beyond a doubt that the infatuated marquis *had* given her a right to his name and fortune. But as the charming Spaniard passed with graceful bows, witty words, and laughing repartees, a general smile appeared on the admiring faces of her friends, for the audacious creature had dressed the little mulatto girl who bore her train, in the same blue and silver brocade, upon which Thyra so prided herself. The point of the joke flashed upon the company at a glance, and they enjoyed it with the zest of Frenchmen.

All eyes followed the rival queens as they met, and all ears were alert to catch the first words which should open the battle. A sudden flush had burned deep on Thyra's fair face, as she saw and understood the insult which Nadine had devised with feminine skill, in return for her own false dealing. But for pride, she could have burst into wrathful tears or vehement reproaches, so intense was her indignation and disgust. The thought of her rival's gratification, in such an open confession of defeat, conquered the first impulse, and gave her courage to control her voice, face, and manner, as the beautiful Spaniard paused before her, saying with a smile that exasperated her almost past endurance:

"Good evening, mademoiselle; you too have changed your mind, regarding your costume. Such caprices are natural, and you are charming in anything. Had I known your plan I could have lent you a magnificent suit, which Gustave's ancestress, a veritable marquise, once wore."

"You are truly amiable, but I am well pleased with the silk which her majesty has approved. Are the pelters the lighter for being made of diamonds," replied Thyra, roused to an unusual degree by the imminence of her peril.

"Infinitely lighter, *ma amie;* the count finds them so attractive on another that he *may* be persuaded to offer similar ones for your acceptance."

The last words were spoken in German, which language the count did not understand. He had followed Nadine with admiring eyes from the moment she entered, and had just offered his arm with a flowery compliment to his "fair countrywoman." Thyra set her teeth as Nadine accepted the honor before her face and sailed away, using her fine eyes and glittering face with the grace and effect of a born Spaniard, while the be-dizened little mulatto smirked behind her, taking an elfish delight in her own temporary importance, and the success of the plot.

"Behold your wish accomplished; the statue is awake, and the little demon has roused her as I foretold," whispered Delmar to Albany, as he nodded toward the deserted one, to whom excitement had given the only charm her beauty lacked.

"She is magnificent. Go and comfort her till I send the count to complete the cure. He cannot fail to surrender if he sees her now. I began to tremble for my money five minutes ago, but I am sure Thyra will win in spite of Nadine's bold stroke."

The good-natured Englishman executed his manœuvre successfully, and devoted himself to Nadine, while the count returned to his allegiance, and soon verified Albany's prediction, by surrendering heart, hand, and fortune to the animated statue.

It was a gay and brilliant little ball, such as the pleasure-loving old marquis well knew how to give, and all went smoothly till after supper. Nadine was standing near her husband when a servant handed her a note. Unaccustomed to the etiquette of her new station, she opened and read it without apology. A strange expression passed over her face as the few words it contained met her eyes, and for a moment she seemed about to tear it up. At that instant Albany's laugh reached her, reminded her of the wager, and banished her hesitation like a spell. Turning to the marquis, she showed the note, whispering in a commanding tone, yet with a caressing touch on his arm:

"It is true, but I am to manage the affair, so be silent, my brave old lion, for I will not have you endanger yourself by exciting his anger."

Appeased by the compliment, the marquis submitted, though he assumed his haughtiest mien as the count was seen approaching, with Thyra on his arm, looking more beautiful than ever.

"Good! He has spoken at last, and she is coming to tell me. I know it by the proud air she assumes. Poor thing, I pity her, but my rank demands that I should resent the insult of this man's presence. Restrain yourself, Gustave, a word will finish the affair."

As she spoke of her rank, Nadine laughed so blithely that those near turned to see the cause of her merriment, and both Thyra and the count smiled involuntarily as they paused before her.

"Thanks for the good omen you give us, madame, for we come to ask your congratulations on a union which we trust may prove as happy as your own," began the count, with a courtly air which set somewhat awkwardly upon him.

In an instant such a sudden change came over Nadine that it startled the observers. The brilliant, mobile face seemed to freeze into a mask, expressive of nothing but the most withering contempt; the smile vanished, the dark brows lowered, the lips curled, and the pose of the whole figure added significance to the haughty gesture with which she drew her trailing laces about her, as if there was contamination in the touch of those who stood before her. Entirely ignoring the count, she fixed her eyes on Thyra with a look which chilled her heart, and said, slowly but distinctly:

"Mademoiselle, you told me this morning that your rank would forbid your visiting me at Vichy; permit me to tell you that *my* rank will render it impossible for me to receive you there, or elsewhere."

"I do not comprehend you, madame," stammered Thyra, feeling that some heavier stroke than any she had yet received was in store for her.

"This note, from one in authority, will convince you that the Marquise de la Faille cannot associate with the *fiancée* of a—convict."

As the last word dropped from the girl's lips, the count wheeled sharply round on the marquis, saying between his teeth:

"Monsieur, I look to you to answer this insult."

"Pardon, I can only fight with gentlemen," replied the old man, with all the tranquil hauteur of a patrician.

Pale to the lips with passion the count lifted his hand to strike, but before the blow could fall, Thyra caught his arm and confronted him with a face of such despair that shame quenched wrath and a guilty fear banished the courage of desperation.

"Is it true?" she said, in a tone that pierced all hearts, as she held the note before him, demanding a reply by the eloquence of her eager eyes and grief-stricken mien.

"It is a lie, and I will prove it so!" he answered, defiantly, but as the words passed his lips, his bold eyes fell before her own, a traitorous flush dyed his swarthy cheek, and an involuntary gesture of the left shoulder betrayed that he had felt the fiery torture of the convict's brand.

With a superb gesture of disdain Thyra pointed to the door, uttering the one word "Go!" with a tragic force that would have made her fortune on the stage; and, as if overwhelmed by her scorn, the *ci-devant* count rushed from the room in guilty silence. For an instant no one spoke; then, turning to Nadine, Thyra added, in a tone full of ominous suggestion:

"For this last kindness rest assured, madame, I shall not long remain your debtor. Since I have ceased to be worthy of the

"With a superb gesture of disdain Thyra pointed to the door, uttering the one word 'Go!'" (The pointing character in the illustration is not Thyra but Nadine — the artist erred.)

honor of your friendship I will at once relieve you of my presence." And with a grand obeisance, full of mock deference, the vanquished queen sailed royally away, leaving the victor but half satisfied at her success.

While waiting for a servant to call her carriage, Thyra paced to and fro along the balcony on which the anteroom opened, trying to assuage the bitterness of her emotions. This balcony ran round the entire wing of the hotel, and, led by an uncontrollable impulse to learn the sentiments of those whom she had quitted, Thyra glided from one open window to another, hearing and seeing enough to nearly madden her. Some laughed

and jested at her disappointment, a few pitied, and many con-
demned her; but nearly all applauded Nadine's success, and ad-
mired the skill and courage with which she had won the
marquis and defeated the count. Coming at length to a window
half-shrouded in flowers, Thyra saw her rival gayly talking with
Albany and Delmar. To the wild eyes steadily watching her she
had never looked so lovely, and as she listened to the words that
followed, Thyra muttered, fiercely:

"I could kill her!"

"But how, in heaven's name, did you discover the man's secret?" asked Albany, rather brusquely, for he had lost his wager.

"I have to thank you, monsieur, for the hint that set me on
the trail," replied Nadine, smiling as she glanced up at him
with eyes full of merry malice.

"Me! I never spoke to you of my suspicions, or the rumors
afloat!" he ejaculated, in surprise.

"The next time you exchange confidences with your friends,
choose a safer place than the myrtle alley, near the 'Restauration
de Dreher,'" laughed Nadine, with a significance which en-
lightened both hearers.

"Then you learned our wager and set yourself to win for me?
Ah, madame, I am your devoted slave forever, for you have done
me a service and proved that I was right in believing that you
would outshine and outmanœuvre this leaden-witted Thyra."

And, as he spoke, Delmar gallantly kissed the pretty hand
that wielded the fan.

At that moment a temptation came to the poor girl listening
there alone in the dark, and she yielded to it, for this cruel rival
had shown her no mercy. One end of Nadine's mantilla had
blown out among the leaves that rustled in the wind; some
peeping servant had left a half-smoked cigarette on the balcony,
and as her eye went from the fiery spark at her feet to the shred

of lace that seemed to flutter tauntingly as it unveiled the round arm lying on the cushions just within, Thyra saw a way to avenge her wrongs, and prove herself the victor in spite of all that had passed. It was the work of an instant to lift the smoldering spark and lay it on the filmy fabric, to watch the breeze fan it to a little flame, and the flame steal on unobserved till the mantilla suddenly blazed up like an awful glory about the fair head of its wearer.

A cry of terror, the sudden flight of a burning figure down the long *salon,* an imploring "Gustave! save me, save me!" a rush of many feet, and then a half-senseless creature lying on the breast of the marquis, who had crushed out the fire in his arms.

"Disfigured for life! disfigured for life!" moaned the poor girl, remembering, even in her torture, the deep scars which would mar forever the beauty of the bosom, arms, and face, which a moment ago had been so fair.

"Yes! now love, rank, success, and youth are all poisoned for you, madame la marquise. Now the diamond fetters will grow heavy while you wear them, and liberty possess no charm when they fall off. *I* preserve my beauty and my freedom still, and it is *I* who win at last!"

The exulting voice rose from the darkness without as a beautiful, desperate face flashed before their startled eyes for a second, and then vanished, never to be seen by them again.

····

Honor's Fortune

Chapter I

SHE STOOD THERE ALONE, face to face with a great temptation, for she held her fate in her hand. Few girls of seventeen would pause long in deciding between sunshine and shadow. As her eye glanced over the ardent letter of her boy-lover, she contrasted the life that would be hers if she fled with him, and the life she must continue to lead if she refused. On one side, love, wealth, pleasure, freedom; on the other, neglect, poverty, distasteful labor, and the bitterest dependence.

She did not truly love young St. John, but his devotion touched and charmed her; her heart was free, and she believed she could easily learn to love if she became his wife. She hated with all the vehemence of a passionate nature the cousin who grudgingly gave the orphan a home, and made the favor hard to accept by reproaches and injustice.

"I shall do something desperate unless I break away, for this dreadful life will kill me," she muttered, as she glanced about the poor room, and the shabby dress that could not hide her beauty. "Gertrude thinks I have no spirit, and believes I will remain her drudge for ever. She fancies I've neither money, sense, nor courage enough to escape; but I have all three. St.

John opens the way, and I'd gladly go if it did not seem wrong to accept his help and marry without love. Poor boy! he is so ardent, and I cannot deny that it is sweet to be loved. There is no other way; I must fly to-night, or wait years, perhaps, for another chance like this."

She stood a moment with her eyes fixed intently on the outer gloom, as if to pierce the future; then a smile broke over her face, and she threw up her hand with a half-triumphant, half-defiant gesture, exclaiming:

"I'll go! Surely with youth, beauty, courage and talent, I can win liberty, and earn the right to enjoy it."

As if afraid her decision might waver, she bestirred herself energetically. A few garments from her scanty wardrobe, and a few little treasures were soon made into a portable parcel. Her plain cloak and bonnet were soon on, and, leaving a note of brief but bitterly ironical thanks for her cousin's kindness, she glided through the silent house out into the autumn night. On the threshold she paused, with a sudden sinking of the heart, for the great world lay before her, unknown, untried, and she was leaving the one refuge she possessed.

As she stood there, a fresh gust blew across the lawn, a brilliant star shone through the flying clouds, and across the silence came the quick tramp of horses' feet, the signal that the hour had come. The free wind, the propitious star, the welcome sound, all cheered her heart, confirmed her courage, and, with a silent gesture, as if she cast off a chain, the girl sprang forward to meet liberty and love.

The carriage waited at the appointed spot, but her lover was not there.

"He was detained by his father's illness, miss; but here's a note saying he'll meet you without fail at Croydon. The night-train gets in at four in the morning, and we shall be there by

two, so there is no danger of missing," said the confidential servant, as respectfully as if she was already his mistress.

Away they went, and for an hour Honor enjoyed the excitement and the romance of the flight with all the zest of a girl.
But, as the time approached when she should meet her lover,
her courage strangely failed, and she almost longed to be safely
back in her dreary room. The thought of that hasty marriage
daunted her, and she began to frame excuses and delays.

By two o'clock she was quietly settled in a room of the Croydon Hotel to await St. John's arrival. Two hours were hers in
which to make or mar her fortune, and, as she paced the
luxurious chamber, she was suddenly inspired with a thought
that opened a way of escape from both the old bondage and
the new.

"How often I have longed to be on my way to London with
money in my purse, and no one to control or counsel me? Now
my wish is granted, and I should enjoy it heartily but for that
poor boy. If I could leave him out I should be entirely content,
and ——"

There she paused, abruptly, for the new thought came filling
her with fresh courage and energy.

"Why not leave him out for a time, at least? Why not go
privately away before he comes, leaving word that he shall hear
from me soon? London is but fifteen miles away; I have ten
pounds in my purse. I remember Madame Paul's address; she
loved her little pupil long ago, and will help me now. I have
heard more than one person tell Gertrude that my voice would
make my fortune; now I'll try it. I'll sing, earn money, repay St.
John, and make my peace. Then, if I can love him, I will; if
not, he'll soon outlive his boyish passion. Come, this is a good
thought; I'll act upon it."

Putting back the curtain, she looked out. A balcony ran

along that side of the hotel; steps descended from one end into a small garden; a low wall shut it from the street, and beyond was the sleeping town, the wide common, with London looming dimly in the distance.

"It is possible," muttered Honor, looking and listening keenly. "Nearly an hour before the train is in; by that time I can be lost in the great park yonder, and take an early train on the other side."

Hastily writing a few lines, she left them on the toilet-table, and stole out to essay a second flight.

Gliding like a shadow past the curtained windows looking on the balcony, she crossed the garden unseen, leaped the low wall, and hastened down the deserted street toward the open country. Once in the park she felt safe, and walked rapidly on in the gray dawn, meeting no one but the deer, who eyed her with mild surprise from their lairs among the fern.

When the sun rose, it shone upon her sitting alone on the wide common, with unwonted color on her cheeks, unwonted light in her eyes, unwonted happiness in her heart. A blissful sense of freedom possessed her, and youth's hopeful spirit made all things fair and possible.

"It is too early yet for the seven train. I'll sit here and rest, and try my voice, for no one can see or hear me, and it must be in order for Madame Paul's criticism," she said, smiling, as she glanced about her in all directions, and saw nothing but a few sheep, heard nothing but the larks singing blithely as they went up. With a music as sweet and effortless her own fine voice rang out as she sung her most difficult airs, and rejoiced to find how perfect her execution was.

Very lovely did she look, that young girl, sitting alone on the wild common. Her bonnet lay by her side; the wind lifted her bright hair from her forehead; the sunshine glittered on its gold, and touched the delicate bloom of her cheeks as she sung, with a smile on her lips and a brilliant light in her violet eyes, fixed on the far-off city where her future lay.

As she ended a sparkling canzonet, a soft sound of applause startled her to her feet. Turning like a frightened doe, she faced a man who had noiselessly approached, and seemed to have been listening delightedly, as he leaned on a mossy stone. He swept off his hat with a smile and a bow of half-playful, half-earnest contrition, saying, gently, and with a foreign accent:

"Pardon, mademoiselle. It was impossible to restrain my admiration; though by not doing so I deprive myself of the rest of this charming matinée."

Honor made no answer, but stood regarding him with the grave scrutiny of a child; for, as her alarm vanished, curiosity awoke.

A slender, swarthy man of five-and-twenty, with lustrous, dark eyes, a thin-lipped, scarlet mouth, under a delicate mustache, luxuriant black hair, and the well-cut features of an Arab. Plain as his dress was, it received an air of elegance from its wearer, and the sinewy, brown hand that held his hat was as small as a woman's. Something in the cordial ring of the voice, the frank gaze of the fine eyes, the whole singularly attractive expression of that peculiar face pleased the girl, and won her confidence. With a little sigh of relief she said, in a tone of satisfaction and pleasure:

"I thought it was that boy. Thank heaven it isn't! I'm glad you came——"

"Unhappy boy, to be so shunned, and thrice happy me, to be so welcomed!" broke in the stranger, as she paused with a sudden blush at his smile and her own words.

"I meant I was glad to meet any one who would tell me the way to the station. I haven't been here for years, and forget the place."

"I am going there. May I show you the way, mademoiselle?"

"Thank you, yes—on one condition," she answered, slowly, for, though irresistibly impelled to trust the stranger, she remembered that she was a runaway.

"I agree to anything," he said, still addressing her with the air which a well-bred man assumes toward a pretty child of the fair sex. Honor liked it, for, with all her strength of character, she was as artless as a little girl.

"Please, don't tell any one you met me. Will you promise that? Indeed, you may. I'm doing no harm, and only leaving those who wrong me," she said, earnestly.

"What a heartless boy, to wrong so sweet a sister! Can nothing be done to make him behave?" he answered, laughing.

"Now, you mistake," she cried, hastily, unconsciously betraying that she was no child. "The boy isn't my brother, and he loves me too well to trouble me. Let him be. It is an unkind woman who drives me away. I'm going to an old friend in London, and I go clandestinely, because I will have liberty. Do you blame me?" she asked, with kindling eyes, yet a wistful look that evidently touched him.

"I love freedom too well myself to blame any one for securing it at all costs. Permit me to offer my help, for you are too young, and—pardon me that I say it to your face—too beautiful to travel alone, mademoiselle."

She shook her head impatiently, but gave no sign of gratified vanity, as she fixed her lovely eyes on his in a grave glance of inquiry that would have aroused in any man a sincere desire to win her confidence. He bore that scrutiny successfully, for, with a sudden smile and an impulsive gesture full of grace, she offered her hand, saying, frankly:

"I trust you, sir. I don't know why I do so, but I am sure you will be an honest friend to me."

"I will."

The hearty brevity of his reply was more emphatic and satisfactory than the most eloquent protestations, and the cordial pressure of the hand was a better pledge than any oath.

"Thank you! Now I must go, for the early train will soon pass. Is it far?" she said, rising, with a sudden consciousness that a night of excitement and fatigue was beginning to tell upon her strength.

"Just over the common—you can see the roof of the station in the valley yonder. No, I carry this, and have still an arm to offer you, my tired comrade," he answered, lifting her parcel, and respectfully proffering the much-needed support.

But Honor shyly declined it, and walked on beside him, finding it very pleasant to be traveling in such courteous company. He smiled, but said nothing, till the girl asked, abruptly, as if following her own thoughts:

"Did you really like my singing?"

"I did. You have a wonderful voice."

"Do you think I could sing for money with any chance of success?" she went on, in a pretty, business-like way that would have amused him had he not been too much interested to observe it.

He glanced at the young face beside him, and a shadow passed over his own as he thought how soon its innocent freshness would disappear in such a life.

"I have no doubt of it. But is that necessary?"

"Why, yes, of course it is," she said, opening her eyes at him, as if surprised at the question. "I've nothing in the world but my voice and a little borrowed money. I wish to support myself, and I'll do anything rather than go back, or marry—some one I don't love."

She checked the name on her lips, and looked abashed that she had allowed so much to escape her. The stranger observed this, and made mental notes, but betrayed no especial interest, and replied, kindly:

"You are right; and, if your friend possess the power to help you, both freedom and independence may be yours."

"I'm glad to hear you say that. I'm very hopeful—very ignorant; but I really wish to help myself, and feel that I can if I am only let alone."

She glanced over her shoulder as she spoke, and uttered a low cry of terror, for several men were rapidly approaching.

"It is he!—St. John! Don't let him take me away! I don't love him; I can't marry him; I'll go back and be miserable rather than do that! Oh, help me—I've no friend but you!"

She clung to his arm as she spoke, with the vehemence of mingled fear and resolution.

"No one shall molest you, my child," he said, soothingly. "Tell me how it is, then I can serve you better."

Breathless with the haste she made, and still holding fast to the strong arm of her new friend, Honor poured out her little story as she went, unconscious of the sudden and entire change which passed over her hearer as he listened.

"Rest tranquil, my girl; I shall protect you. See, the station is here, and the train already approaches. Hold fast, and we shall be there in time to escape those persons."

Casting a quick glance behind him, the stranger strode on, half carrying Honor. Just as the train thundered up, they reached the platform, and, with a word to the guard, they sprang into an empty carriage. No other passengers waited at the little station, and they rolled away before the pursuers, if such they were, appeared in sight.

Pale and panting, Honor lay back, quite spent with this last flurry. She dimly wondered at the exulting laugh which broke from her companion as they shot away, and was touched by the gentle care he took of her, trying by every reassuring wile to cheer and restore her. She was soon herself again, and during that brief journey she permitted him to draw from her the story of her past life.

"Papa died long ago, and mamma offended Uncle Hugh by refusing to marry him. He went away to India, and we knew no more of him till two or three years ago he sent word that he was coming home, and the niece who was the best in every way should be his heiress. There is only Cousin Gertrude and myself, and of course he will choose her, for she has written him all sorts of bad reports of me, and tried in every way to win his favor. I don't care much for his money, but I do long for his love, I've had so little since mamma died."

"Why did you not write also, and set the matter straight with the old man?" asked the stranger, as she paused with trembling lips.

"I did, but my letters were not allowed to go. I tried to do well, and live on patiently till uncle came; but Gertrude was so tyrannical and unkind I could not bear it. She is a widow now, and I taught her children, but she wouldn't let them love me, and I was miserable. Then St. John saw me by accident, and loved me. Gertrude refused him, but he managed to write, and so it came about that I ran away. If I only cared for him I should not leave him; but I don't, and every hour makes me surer of it. Am I doing very wrong to disappoint the poor boy?"

"How old is the boy?" asked her companion, knitting his brows, though an amused smile lurked about his mouth.

"Nineteen," she answered, coloring; then she broke into a silvery laugh, and exclaimed, with charming frankness, "I know it must sound very childish and silly, and I dare say I am outraging all the proprieties by running away twice, and telling all my affairs to an utter stranger. But I've been so shut up, I know no more of the world than a child, and I really can't help trusting you, sir, you are so kind."

"Thank you. I'll prove worthy of your confidence, Miss Honor," began the stranger; but the girl exclaimed, abruptly:

"How do you know my name? I didn't tell you?"

He bit his lip, his brown cheek flushed a little, and his keen eye seemed to glance over her with a half-scrutinizing, half annoyed expression. Then a quick smile appeared, and with an air of relief he touched the handkerchief that lay in her lap, saying, quietly:

"I read it there."

"What sharp eyes you must have! The words are almost washed out," and the girl gravely examined the corner of the handkerchief.

He smiled, and changed the subject, and beguiled the way so pleasantly that Honor was surprised when the journey ended. The noise and bustle at the Waterloo Station so bewildered her that she gratefully permitted her new friend to take care of her. Placing her in a cab, he gave Madame Paul's address to the man, pressed her hand, and said, emphatically:

"I do not say adieu, because I shall see you again. In any trouble send to me, and remember I am your friend. Here is my address. Be of good courage, little Honor; you will find your fortune soon."

With a smile that seemed to prophesy all good things, he

vanished, leaving a card in her hand, bearing the words, "H. Tarifa, St. James Hotel, London."

Chapter II

A WEEK LATER a similar card was carried up to Mrs. Gertrude Avon, and threw that lady into a state of joyful excitement.

"News from Uncle Hugh. This is the name of his partner in Calcutta. Perhaps he is coming. How fortunate that Honor has lost all hope of the fortune! Is this H. Tarifa an old man, Annette?" she asked of her maid, who was helping her to give a few effective touches to her dress.

"No, madame—young, and very handsome."

"Ah! the son, doubtless. Give me the wrapper trimmed with Valenciennes, and let down a few more curls. They give a youthful look to my face."

The ten minutes' delay caused by Mrs. Avon's desire to make a coquettish toilet cost her more than she knew; for while he waited, her guest strolled about the room, using his keen eyes to some purpose. A card with these words penciled under St. John's name was one discovery: "She is at Madame P.'s, but will not see me." A portrait of Mrs. Avon caused him to mutter, after a long survey, "Insincere eyes, and a hard mouth. Poor little Honor must have fared ill in the hands of such a woman." And the prattle of a child playing in the room, whom he questioned, brought out the fact that Honor was much beloved and mourned by her little pupils.

With a soft rustle, a beaming smile, and a white hand hospitably extended, Mrs. Avon glided into the room, paused with well-acted surprise, dropped her fine eyes, and murmured, with charming embarrassment:

"Pardon me. I fancied my dear uncle's partner would be an older man. Nevertheless, permit me to welcome you to England for his sake."

M. Tarifa bowed, and replied, in a cool, calm tone, which made Mrs. Avon look keenly at him:

"I am now the only remaining member of the old firm, my father having retired and your uncle being dead. Excuse my abrupt announcement of the fact; but the letters dispatched before I sailed were evidently lost, therefore I find you unprepared for the sad news."

"Yes," sighed Mrs. Avon, from behind her handkerchief, which she had lifted to hide, not tears, but exultation that the fortune was so near her grasp. "I will not detain you by any selfish grief, for I loved the old man, though we have been parted so long."

"I fear that I have yet another disappointment for you, madame; but perhaps your knowledge of your uncle's whims may have prepared you for any caprice of his. What caused the sudden change of purpose, I cannot tell, unless it was gratitude for a small favor I once did him; but when his will was read, it appeared that his whole fortune was left to me."

"You!" and Mrs. Avon's eyes flashed with irrepressible anger at the downfall of all her hopes.

"To me, with no mention of his nieces, except a wish which I find it somewhat difficult to mention, though far less difficult to obey than I had expected."

Something in the tone of the young man's voice, the smile that touched his lips, and the softened glance of his brilliant southern eyes caused a sudden hope to spring up in the woman's heart. Vailing her sharp disappointment under a half-timid, half-melancholy air, she said, sweetly:

"Believe me, I rejoice at your prosperity, and am sure that

you will pardon a mother's regret at the loss which affects her fatherless children. May I ask what my uncle's wish was?"

"That I should share the fortune with one of his lawful heirs by marrying her."

"How cruel of him to hamper his bequest with so hard a condition!" and Mrs. Avon gave him an eloquent look as she spoke.

"Not hard, but every moment growing easier," gallantly replied M. Tarifa. "If you will permit me to make a few inquiries concerning your sister,* I shall be better able to conduct this delicate affair. She is with you, I believe?"

"Alas, no; she eloped a week ago, and is now married, I hope."

"You know nothing of her, then?"

"Nothing, except that she rejected my love and protection, and left me for a wild boy, who will soon desert her, I fear."

"If so, you will receive and protect her again?"

"Never! How can I, with my little daughters growing up about me? I pity her; but I must think of them, for I have no one to lean upon, and, though five years a widow, I have not yet learned to bear my solitude with courage."

"I may then regard Miss Honor as no longer worthy a share of your uncle's benefaction?"

"I leave that for you to decide," and Mrs. Avon's scornful face plainly expressed her opinion.

There was a little pause, in which M. Tarifa seemed lost in thought, as he sat looking at the handsome woman before him. She fancied he was embarrassed at the position in which he

---

* Although their precise relationship is not significant to the plot, the sudden mid-story transformation of cousin Gertrude into Honor's sister is a careless authorial lapse.

found himself, and she came to his assistance with an artful question:

"May I ask if this singular desire of the old man is in any way binding upon you, sir?"

"Not in the least; but I desire to show my gratitude by complying with it, if possible. I am anxious to settle in England, to make a home for my father, and find happiness for myself. Being heart-free, and having seen pictures of both nieces, the task seemed full of romance to me, and I came, hoping to prosper in the only means of restitution which it is in my power to make. But as Miss Honor is lost, there is no hope of success, perhaps; at least, I dare not believe so, unless——"

As the last words fell slowly from his lips, Mrs. Avon, colored with soft confusion, dropped her eyes, and tenderly caressing the child leaning on her knee, she murmured, in a low tone:

"It is so very sudden and unexpected—such an embarrassing position—I would do much for my darling. My first marriage was a loveless one, but I have honored my husband's memory by a long widowhood. In time I might find my loneliness too hard to bear. Indeed, I need a friend. Be that to me at least, and ask nothing more as yet!"

As a piece of acting, that speech was perfect, and would have touched any man but the one who heard it. Being forewarned, he was forearmed, and a satirical smile passed across his face as he answered, in a voice to which a softer language than ours lent its music:

"Thank you for that permission. I promised to befriend the old man's niece, and I will. I may come again?" he added, rising.

"Yes," was all she said, but her eyes bade him welcome so

eloquently that he could not doubt the sincerity of her invitation.

"And your unhappy sister, is there no way in which I can aid her?" he asked, pausing, with a significant look.

"If she is Mrs. St. John, she will need no help. If she is not, I no longer have a sister. Of course, you are at liberty to do what you will; but remember that you choose between us, for I decline all further friendship, if those reckless children are to be taken up after the disgrace they have brought upon me."

"My dear Mrs. Avon, have no fears. My choice is already made," and kissing her hand in his graceful foreign fashion, M. Tarifa took his leave, wearing an expression of satisfaction which both puzzled and charmed the ambitious widow.

For three weeks the young millionaire came and went, always with some pretext of business to prevent awkwardness in the interviews, which were always very brief, in spite of Mrs. Avon's fascinations.

"He is young," she thought, "and has seen little of women, evidently. This coldness is assumed for my sake. A man with such eyes and voice must be full of fire and tenderness. A little patience and his passion will break out, and then what a magnificent lover he will be! Thank heaven Honor destroyed her chance of winning before he came, for her blue eyes would surely have bewitched him."

One thing struck Mrs. Avon, which was, that at each visit M. Tarifa alluded to her sister; but she fancied that the girl's picture had awakened an interest in the young man's mind, and set herself to efface it as fast as possible by artfully-worded insinuations, accusations, and regrets; all of which were received in grave silence, and with a look of satisfaction which delighted her.

On the fourth week he arrived, radiant with some new happiness, which made him so charming that Mrs. Avon felt that the long-desired moment must be at hand when the lover's ardor was to replace the stranger's natural reserve.

"I have a favor to ask of you—may I say Gertrude?" he began, with a new softness in both face and tone.

"You know you may. What favor, Henri?" and the widow uttered his name with the timid tenderness of a young girl.

"I want you to forgive your sister."

"Never till she is married."

"She is married."

"Who told you that?" and the widow's shyness vanished, as she put the question sharply.

"I saw it done," was the cool reply.

"You! When?—where?—why?"

"Two days ago, at Madame Paul's, and because I felt that the young creature needed a protector."

"And that boy actually married her? Truly, it was the least he could do after the wrong he had done her."

"He felt that, and gladly made the only reparation in his power," replied Tarifa, with a tranquil smile.

"How good you are! That sad affair needed a wise and energetic head to settle it, and in the midst of your own duties you found time to do it. I hope they were truly grateful. I never can thank you for your brotherly care of that headstrong girl;" and Mrs. Avon put both her white hands in his with a tender look.

"They *were* very grateful, and if you will promise to pardon them, I shall consider your debt to me well paid."

"Anything for you, Henri," whispered the widow.

"Thanks! And will you receive them to-morrow for my sake, Gertrude?"

"'Here is the bridegroom, Gerty,' and Honor turned to fold both hands tenderly about the arm of Tarifa."

"I will, and gladly forget and forgive the past. Does that satisfy you?"

"Entirely. Now I must leave you; but when I come again receive me with a smile like this, and find that virtue is always its own reward."

Mrs. Avon's toilet was a marvel of taste, and Mrs. Avon's face wore its sweetest smiles as she rose to greet her guests next day, when Tarifa led her lovely sister in to be embraced with well-acted affection and delight.

"Where is the bridegroom? Does he fear to face me? Ah, well he may, after robbing me of my darling; but I have promised to pardon everything, and will keep my word for your sake,

Henri," she said, longing to have the scene over, that she might receive the reward.

"Here is the bridegroom, Gerty," and Honor turned to fold both hands tenderly about the arm of Tarifa, who looked the lover to the life now.

"You! It is a lie!" cried Mrs. Avon, in a tone of despair, for his face answered before his lips.

"You told me to choose between you, and I did so. I gave you many opportunities to save your sister, but you rejected them all, to your own loss. I loved her image before I found the fair reality waiting for me on the moor, and when you cast her off, my heart took her in. If the old man wronged her, I have atoned for it by giving her all I possess."

"And she—that imprudent child has won the fortune, after all," gasped Mrs. Avon, as her last hope vanished.

"The only fortune that I covet is here," and Honor leaned her bright head on her husband's breast, thinking only of the generous and tender heart that took her in when most forlorn.

. . . . .

___

My Mysterious Mademoiselle

A̲t lyons i engaged a coupé, laid in a substantial
lunch, got out my novels and cigars, and prepared to make myself as comfortable as circumstances permitted; for we should
not reach Nice till morning, and a night journey was my especial detestation. Nothing would have induced me to undertake
it in mid-winter, but a pathetic letter from my sister, imploring
me to come to her, as she was failing fast, and had a precious
gift to bestow upon me before she died. This sister had mortally
offended our father by marrying a Frenchman. The old man
never forgave her, never would see her, and cut her off with a
shilling in his will. I had been forbidden to have any communi-
cation with her on pain of disinheritance, and had obeyed, for I
shared my father's prejudice, and made no attempt to befriend
my sister, even when I learned that she was a widow, although
my father's death freed me from my promise. For more than
fifteen years we had been utterly estranged; but when her pleading letter came to me, my heart softened, and I longed to see
her. My conscience reproached me, and, leaving my cozy bach-
elor establishment in London, I hurried away, hoping to repair
the neglect of years by tardy tenderness and care.

My thoughts worried me that night, and the fear of being

too late haunted me distressfully. I could neither read, sleep, nor smoke, and soon heartily wished I had taken a seat in a double carriage, where society of some sort would have made the long hours more endurable. As we stopped at a way-station, I was roused from a remorseful reverie by the guard, who put in his head to inquire, with an insinuating shrug and smile:

"Will monsieur permit a lady to enter? The train is very full, and no place remains for her in the first-class. It will be a great kindness if monsieur will take pity on the charming little mademoiselle."

He dropped his voice in uttering the last words, and gave a nod, which plainly expressed his opinion that monsieur would not regret the courtesy. Glad to be relieved from the solitude that oppressed me, I consented at once, and waited with some curiosity to see what sort of companion I was to have for the next few hours.

The first glance satisfied me; but, like a true Englishman, I made no demonstration of interest beyond a bow and a brief reply to the apologies and thanks uttered in a fresh young voice as the new-comer took her seat. A slender girl of sixteen or so, simply dressed in black, with a little hat tied down over golden curls, and a rosy face, lit up by lustrous hazel eyes, at once arch, modest and wistful. A cloak and a plump traveling bag were all her luggage, and quickly arranging them, she drew out a book, sank back in her corner, and appeared to read, as if anxious to render me forgetful of her presence as soon as possible.

I liked that, and resolved to convince her at the first opportunity that I was no English bear, but a gentleman who could be very agreeable when he chose.

The opportunity did not arrive as soon as I hoped, and I began to grow impatient to hear the fresh young voice again. I made a few attempts at conversation, but the little girl seemed timid, for she answered in the briefest words, and fell to reading again, forcing me to content myself with admiring the long curled lashes, the rosy mouth, and the golden hair of this demure demoiselle.

She was evidently afraid of the big, black-bearded gentleman, and would not be drawn out, so I solaced myself by watching her in the windows opposite, which reflected every movement like a mirror.

Presently the book slipped from her hand, the bright eyes grew heavy, the pretty head began to nod, and sleep grew more and more irresistible. Half closing my eyes, I feigned slumber, and was amused at the little girl's evident relief. She peeped at first, then took a good look, then smiled to herself as if well pleased, yawned, and rubbed her eyes like a sleepy child, took off her hat, tied a coquettish rose-colored rigolette over her soft hair, viewed herself in the glass, and laughed a low laugh, so full of merriment, that I found it difficult to keep my countenance. Then, with a roguish glance at me, she put out her hand toward the flask of wine lying on the leaf, with a half-open case of chocolate croquettes, which I had been munching, lifted the flask to her lips, put it hastily down again, took one bon-bon, and, curling herself up like a kitten, seemed to drop asleep at once.

"Poor little thing," I thought to myself, "she is hungry, cold, and tired; she longs for a warm sip, a sugar-plum, and a kind word, I dare say. She is far too young and pretty to be traveling alone. I must take care of her."

In pursuance of which friendly resolve I laid my rug lightly over her, slipped a soft shawl under her head, drew the curtains for warmth, and then repaid myself for these attentions by looking long and freely at the face encircled by the rosy cloud. Prettier than ever when flushed with sleep did it look, and I quite lost myself in the pleasant reverie which came to me while leaning over the young girl, watching the silken lashes lying quietly on the blooming cheeks, listening to her soft breath, touching the yellow curls that strayed over the arm of the seat, and wondering who the charming little person might be. She reminded me of my first sweetheart—a pretty cousin, who had captivated my boyish heart at eighteen, and dealt it a wound it never could forget. At five-and-thirty these little romances sometimes return to one's memory fresher and dearer for the years that have taught us the sweetness of youth—the bitterness of regret. In a sort of waking dream I sat looking at the stranger, who seemed to wear the guise of my first love, till suddenly the great eyes flashed wide open, the girl sprung up, and, clasping her hands, cried, imploringly:

"Ah, monsieur, do not hurt me, for I am helpless. Take my little purse; take all I have, but spare my life for my poor mother's sake!"

"Good heavens, child, do you take me for a robber?" I exclaimed, startled out of my sentimental fancies by this unexpected performance.

"Pardon; I was dreaming; I woke to find you bending over me, and I was frightened," she murmured, eying me timidly.

"That was also a part of your dream. Do I look like a rascal, mademoiselle?" I demanded, anxious to reassure her.

"Indeed, no; you look truly kind, and I trust you. But I am not used to traveling alone; I am anxious and timid, yet now I do not fear. Pardon, monsieur; pray, pardon a poor child who has no friend to protect her."

She put out her hand with an impulsive gesture, as the soft

"Ah, monsieur, do not hurt me, for I am helpless. Take my little purse; take all I have, but spare my life!"

eyes were lifted confidingly to mine, and what could I do but kiss the hand in true French style, and smile back into the eyes with involuntary tenderness, as I replied, with unusual gallantry:

"Not without a friend to protect her, if mademoiselle will permit me the happiness. Rest tranquil, no one shall harm you. Confide in me, and you shall find that we 'cold English' have hearts, and may be trusted."

"Ah, so kind, so pitiful! A thousand thanks; but do not let me disturb monsieur. I will have no more panics, and can only atone for my foolish fancy by remaining quiet, that monsieur may sleep."

"Sleep! Not I; and the best atonement you can make is to join me at supper, and wile away this tedious night with friendly confidences. Shall it be so, mademoiselle?" I asked, assuming a paternal air to reassure her.

"That would be pleasant; for I confess I am hungry, and have nothing with me. I left in such haste I forgot——" She paused suddenly, turned scarlet, and drooped her eyes, as if on the point of betraying some secret.

I took no notice, but began to fancy that my little friend was engaged in some romance which might prove interesting. Opening my traveling-case, I set forth cold chicken, *tartines,* wine, and sweetmeats, and served her as respectfully as if she had been a duchess, instead of what I suspected—a run-away school-girl. My manner put her at her ease, and she chatted away with charming frankness, though now and then she checked some word on her lips, blushed and laughed, and looked so merry and mysterious, that I began to find my school-girl a most captivating companion. The hours flew rapidly now; remorse and anxiety slept; I felt blithe and young again, for my lost love seemed to sit beside me; I forgot my years, and almost fancied myself an ardent lad again.

What mademoiselle thought of me I could only guess; but look, tone and manner betrayed the most flattering confidence. I enjoyed the little adventure without a thought of consequences.

At Toulon we changed cars, and I could not get a coupé, but fortunately found places in a carriage, whose only occupant was a sleepy old woman. As I was about taking my seat, after bringing my companion a cup of hot coffee, she uttered an exclamation, dragged her vail over her face, and shrunk into the corner of our compartment.

"What alarms you?" I asked, anxiously, for her mystery piqued my curiosity.

"Look out and see if a tall young man is not promenading the platform, and looking into every carriage," returned mademoiselle, in good English, for the first time.

I looked out, saw the person described, watched him approach, and observed that he glanced eagerly into each car as he passed.

"He is there, and is about to favor us with an inspection. What are your commands, mademoiselle?" I asked.

"Oh, sir, befriend me; cover me up; say that I am ill; call yourself my father for a moment—I will explain it all. Hush, he is here!" and the girl clung to my arm with a nervous gesture, an imploring look, which I could not resist.

The stranger appeared, entered with a grave bow, seated himself opposite, and glanced from me to the muffled figure at my side. We were off in a moment, and no one spoke, till a little cough behind the vail gave the new-comer a pretext for addressing me.

"Mademoiselle is annoyed by the air; permit me to close the window."

"Madame is an invalid, and will thank you to do so," I replied, taking a malicious satisfaction in disobeying the girl, for the idea of passing as her father disgusted me, and I preferred a more youthful title.

A sly pinch of the arm was all the revenge she could take; and, as I stooped to settle the cloaks about her, I got a glance from the hazel eyes, reproachful, defiant, and merry.

"Ah, she has spirit, this little wandering princess. Let us see what our friend opposite has to do with her," I said to myself, feeling almost jealous of the young man, who was a handsome, resolute-looking fellow, in a sort of uniform.

"Does he understand English, madame, my wife?" I whispered to the girl.

"Not a word," she whispered back, with another charming pinch.

"Good; then tell me all about him. I demand an explanation."

"Not now; not here, wait a little. Can you not trust me, when I confide so much to you?"

"No, I am burning with curiosity, and I deserve some reward for my good behavior. Shall I not have it, *ma amie?*"

"Truly, you do, and I will give you anything by-and-by," she began.

"*Anything?*" I asked, quickly.

"Yes; I give you my word."

"I shall hold you to your promise. Come, we will make a little bargain. I will blindly obey you till we reach Nice, if you will frankly tell me the cause of all this mystery before we part."

"Done!" cried the girl, with an odd laugh.

"Done!" said I, feeling that I was probably making a fool of myself.

The young man eyed us sharply as we spoke, but said nothing, and, wishing to make the most of my bargain, I pillowed my little wife's head on my shoulder, and talked in whispers, while she nestled in shelter of my arm, and seemed to enjoy the escapade with all the thoughtless *abandon* of a girl. Why she went off into frequent fits of quiet laughter I did not quite understand, for my whispers were decidedly more tender than witty; but I fancied it hysterical, and, having made up my mind that some touching romance was soon to be revealed to me, I prepared myself for it, by playing my part with spirit, finding something very agreeable in my new *rôle* of devoted husband.

The remarks of our neighbors amused us immensely; for, the old lady, on waking, evidently took us for an English couple on a honeymoon trip, and confided her opinion of the "mad English" to the young man, who knit his brows and mused moodily.

To our great satisfaction, both of our companions quitted us at midnight; and the moment the door closed behind them, the girl tore off her vail, threw herself on the seat opposite me, and laughed till the tears rolled down her cheeks.

"Now, mademoiselle, I demand an explanation," I said, seriously, when her merriment subsided.

"You shall have it; but first tell me what do I look like?" and she turned her face toward me with a wicked smile, that puzzled me more than her words.

"Like a very charming young lady who has run way from school or *pension,* either to escape from a lover or to meet one."

"My faith! but that is a compliment to my skill," muttered the girl, as if to herself; then aloud, and soberly, though her eyes still danced with irrepressible mirth: "Monsieur is right in one thing. I have run away from school, but not to meet or fly a lover. Ah, no; I go to find my mother. She is ill; they concealed it from me; I ran away, and would have walked from Lyons to Nice if old Justine had not helped me."

"And this young man—why did you dread him?" I asked, eagerly.

"He is one of the teachers. He goes to find and reclaim me; but, thanks to my disguise, and your kindness, he has not discovered me."

"But why should he reclaim you? Surely, if your mother is ill, you have a right to visit her, and she would desire it."

"Ah, it is a sad story! I can only tell you that we are poor. I am too young yet to help my mother. Two rich aunts placed me in a fine school, and support me till I am eighteen, on condition that my mother does not see me. They hate her, and I would have rejected their charity, but for the thought that soon I can earn my bread and support her. She wished me to go, and I obeyed, though it broke my heart. I study hard. I suffer many trials. I make no complaint; but I hope and wait, and when the time comes I fly to her, and never leave her any more."

What had come to the girl? The words poured from her lips with impetuous force; her eyes flashed; her face glowed; her voice was possessed with strange eloquence, by turns tender, defiant, proud, and pathetic. She clinched her hands, and dashed her little hat at her feet with a vehement gesture when speaking of her aunts. Her eyes shone through indignant tears when alluding to her trials; and, as she said, brokenly, "I fly to her, and never leave her any more," she opened her arms as if to embrace and hold her mother fast.

It moved me strangely; for, instead of a shallow, coquettish school-girl, I found a passionate, resolute creature, ready to do and dare anything for the mother she loved. I resolved to see the end of this adventure, and wished my sister had a child as fond and faithful to comfort and sustain her; but her only son had died a baby, and she was alone, for I had deserted her.

"Have you no friends but these cruel aunts?" I asked, compassionately.

"No, not one. My father is dead, my mother poor and ill, and I am powerless to help her," she answered, with a sob.

"Not quite; remember I am a friend."

As I spoke I offered my hand; but, to my intense surprise, the girl struck it away from her with a passionate motion, saying, almost fiercely:

"No; it is too late—too late! You should have come before."

"My poor child, calm yourself. I *am* indeed a friend; believe it, and let me help you. I can sympathize with your distress, for I, too, go to Nice to find one dear to me. My poor sister, whom I have neglected many years; but now I go to ask pardon, and to serve her with all my heart. Come, then, let us comfort one another, and go hopefully to meet those who love and long for us."

Still another surprise; for, with a face as sweetly penitent as it had been sternly proud before, this strange girl caught my hand in hers, kissed it warmly, and whispered, gratefully:

"I often dreamed of a friend like this, but never thought to find him so. God bless you, my——" She paused there, hid her face an instant, then looked up without a shadow in her eyes, saying more quietly, and with a smile I could not understand:

"What shall I give you to prove my thanks for your kindness to me?"

"When we part, you shall give me an English good-by."

"A kiss on the lips! Fie! monsieur will not demand that of me," cried the girl, whose changeful face was gay again.

"And, why not, since I am old enough to be called your father."

"Ah, that displeased you! Well, you had your revenge; rest content with that, *mon mari,*" laughed the girl, retreating to a corner with a rebellious air.

"I shall claim my reward when we part; so resign yourself, mademoiselle. By-the-way, what name has my little friend?"

"I will tell you when I pay my debt. Now let me sleep. I am tired, and so are you. Good-night, Monsieur George Vane," and, leaving me to wonder how she had learned my name, the tormenting creature barricaded herself with cloaks and bags, and seemed to sleep tranquilly.

Tired with the long night, I soon dropped off into a doze, which must have been a long one; for, when I woke, I found myself in the dark.

"Where the deuce are we?" I exclaimed; for the lamp was out, and no sign of dawn visible, though I had seen a ruddy streak when I last looked out.

"In the long tunnel near Nice," answered a voice from the gloom.

"Ah, mademoiselle is awake! Is she not afraid that I may demand payment now?"

"Wait till the light comes, and if you deserve it *then,* you shall have it," and I heard the little gipsy laughing in her corner. The next minute a spark glowed opposite me; the odor of my choice cigarettes filled the air, and the crackle of a bon-bon was heard.

Before I could make up my mind how to punish these freaks, we shot out of the tunnel, and I sat petrified with amazement, for there, opposite me, lounged, not my pretty blonde school-girl, but a handsome black-haired, mischievous lad, in the costume of a pupil of a French military academy; with his little cap rakishly askew, his blue coat buttoned smartly to the chin, his well-booted feet on the seat beside him, and his small hands daintily gloved, this young rascal lay staring at me with such a world of fun in his fine eyes, that I tingled all over with a shock of surprise which almost took my breath away.

"Have a light, uncle?" was the cool remark that broke the long silence.

"Where is the girl?" was all I could say, with a dazed expression.

"There, sir," pointing to the bag, with a smile that made me feel as if I was not yet awake, so like the girl's was it.

"And who the devil are you?" I cried, getting angry all at once.

Standing as straight as an arrow, the boy answered, with a military salute:

"George Vane Vandeleur, at your service, uncle."

"My sister has no children; her boy died years ago, you young villain."

"He tried to, but they wouldn't let him. I'm sorry to contradict you, sir; but I'm your sister's son, and that will prove it."

Much bewildered, I took the letter he handed me, and found it impossible to doubt the boy's word. It was from my sister to her son, telling him that she had written to me, that I had answered kindly, and promised to come to her. She bade the boy visit her if possible, that I might see him, for she could not doubt that I would receive him for her sake, and free him from dependence on the French aunts who made their favors burdensome by reproach and separation.

As I read, I forgave the boy his prank, and longed to give him a hearty welcome; but recollections of my own part in that night's masquerade annoyed me so much that to conceal my chagrin I assumed a stern air, and demanded, coldly:

"Was it necessary to make a girl of yourself in order to visit your mother?"

"Yes, sir," answered the boy, promptly, adding, with the most engaging frankness: "I'll tell you how it was, uncle, and I know you will pardon me, because mamma has often told me of your pranks when a boy, and I made you my hero. See, then, mamma sends me this letter, and I am wild to go, that I may embrace her and see my uncle. But my aunts say, 'No,' and tell them at school that I am to be kept close. Ah, they are strict there; the boys are left no freedom, and my only chance was the one holiday when I go to my aunts. I resolved to run away, and walk to mamma, for nothing shall part us but her will. I had a little money, and I confided my plan to Justine, my old nurse. She is a brave one! She said:

"'You shall go, but not as a beggar. See, I have money. Take it, my son, and visit your mother like a gentleman.'

"That was grand; but I feared to be caught before I could leave Lyons, so I resolved to disguise myself, and then if they followed I should escape them. Often at school I have played girl-parts, because I am small, and have as yet no beard. So Justine dressed me in the skirt, cloak and hat of her granddaughter. I had the blonde wig I wore on the stage, a little rouge, a soft tone, a modest air, and—*voilà mademoiselle!*"

"Exactly; it was well done, though at times you forgot the 'modest air,' nephew," I said, with as much dignity as suppressed merriment permitted.

"It was impossible to remember it at all times; and you did not seem to like mademoiselle the less for a little coquetry," replied the rogue, with a sly glance out of the handsome eyes that had bewitched me.

"Continue your story, sir. Was the young man we met really a teacher?"

"Yes, uncle; but you so kindly protected me that he could not even suspect your delicate wife."

The boy choked over the last word, and burst into a laugh so irresistibly infectious that I joined him, and lost my dignity for ever.

"George, you are a scapegrace," was the only reproof I had breath enough to make.

"But uncle pardons me, since he gives me my name, and looks at me so kindly that I must embrace him."

And with a demonstrative affection which an English boy would have died rather than betray, my French nephew threw his arms about my neck, and kissed me heartily on both cheeks. I had often ridiculed the fashion, but now I rather liked it, and began to think my prejudice ill-founded, as I listened to the lad's account of the sorrows and hardships they had been called on to suffer since his father died.

"Why was I never told of your existence?" I asked, feeling how much I had lost in my long ignorance of this bright boy, who was already dear to me.

"When I was so ill while a baby, mamma wrote to my grand-father, hoping to touch his heart; but he never answered her, and she wrote no more. If uncle had cared to find his nephew, he might easily have done so; the channel is not very wide."

The reproach in the last words went straight to my heart; but I only said, stroking the curly head:

"Did you never mean to make yourself known to me? When your mother was suffering, could you not try me?"

"I never could beg, even for her, and trusted to the good God, and we were helped. I did mean to make myself known to you when I had done something to be proud of; not before."

I knew where that haughty spirit came from, and was as glad to see it as I was to see how much the boy resembled my once lovely sister.

"How did you know me, George?" I asked, finding pleasure in uttering the familiar name, unspoken since my father died.

"I saw your name on your luggage at Marseilles, and thought you looked like the picture mamma cherishes so tenderly, and I resolved to try and touch your heart before you knew who I was. The guard put me into your coupé, for I bribed him, and then I acted my best; but it was so droll I nearly spoiled it all by some boy's word, or a laugh. My faith, uncle, I did not know the English were so gallant."

"It did not occur to you that I might be acting also, perhaps? I own I was puzzled at first, but I soon made up my mind that you were some little adventuress out on a lark, as we say in England, and I behaved accordingly."

"If all little adventuresses got on as well as I did, I fancy many would go on this lark of yours. A talent for acting runs in the family, that is evident," said the boy.

"Hold your tongue, jackanapes!" sternly. "How old are you, my lad?" mildly.

"Fifteen, sir."

"That young to begin the world, with no friends but two cold-hearted old women!"

"Ah, no, I have the good God and my mother, and now— may I say an uncle who loves me a little, and permits me to love him with all my heart?"

Never mind what answer I made; I have recorded weaknesses enough already, so let that pass, as well as the conversation which left both pair of eyes a little wet, but both pair of hearts very happy.

As the train thundered into the station at Nice, just as the sun rose gloriously over the blue Mediterranean, George whispered to me, with the irrepressible impudence of a mischief-loving boy:

"Uncle, shall I give you 'the English good-by' now?"

"No, my lad; give me a hearty English welcome, and God bless you!" I answered, as we shook hands, manfully, and walked away together, laughing over the adventure with my mysterious mademoiselle.

Betrayed by a Buckle

It WAS A BITTER DISAPPOINTMENT, after years of poverty, to find the fortune which I had thought my own suddenly wrested from me by a stranger. I was my uncle's legal heir, for he died childless, as all the world believed, and on hearing of the old man's death, I forgave him his long neglect, and waited eagerly to receive the welcome news of my good fortune. To my dismay, the lawyers wrote me that a daughter had appeared, whose claim could neither be doubted nor set aside; the property was rightfully hers, and I was a poor artist still.

Years ago I had heard of my uncle's marriage, and the birth and death of a little child; he himself died suddenly and left no will, but his last words were:

"Be just—give all to Cecil," and those about him believed that he meant me till this beautiful girl appeared, claiming to be his child, and proving that her name was Cecelia, which gave a new meaning to those last words, uttered with great earnestness and evident distress of mind.

The girl made out her case and won it, for I was too poor to fight against such odds, and all was settled before I could earn enough to leave Italy for home. I resolved to see this unknown cousin before I relinquished all hope, however, for a hint dropped by my old lawyer suggested the possibility of yet winning a share at least of my uncle's handsome fortune.

I was young, comely, accomplished, and the possessor of a good name, to which my talent had already added some honor. Why not woo this bonny cousin, and still be master of the wealth I had been taught to think my own?

The romance of the thing pleased me, and as soon as my engagements permitted I was in England. Desiring to judge for myself, after hearing the dry facts from the lawyers, I went down to the hall, unannounced, meaning to play the unknown artist till satisfied that it was wise to confess the truth.

Armed with a note of introduction from a friend of my uncle's, I presented myself as one desirous of copying a certain fine Titian in the gallery. Miss Stanhope was out, but I was permitted to examine the pictures while awaiting her return. Among the old family portraits was a half-finished one, evidently the young mistress, and I examined it with eagerness.

A very lovely face, yet something marred its beauty. At first I thought it was my own prejudice; but setting aside any natural bitterness of feeling, and regarding it as a work of art alone, I could not escape from the odd fancy that those imperious eyes could flash with a baleful light, that smiling, red mouth might betray with a kiss, and that dimpled hand lead a man to perdition. The warm brown of the luxuriant hair, the smooth curves of the uncovered neck and arms, and the soft, rich coloring of the dress gave a sumptuous and seductive grace to the well-painted picture, the charm of which I felt in spite of myself.

Quite forgetting the Titian, I leaned back in the depths of a luxurious couch, with my eyes fixed on the likeness of my future wife, as I already called my cousin, in the reverie to which I surrendered myself.

A low laugh startled me to my feet, and made me stare in

dumb surprise at the apparition before me. The picture seemed to have stepped from its frame, for there in the arched doorway against a background of soft gloom was Miss Stanhope. The same imperious eyes fixed full upon me, the red lips smiling archly, the floating hair, half golden in the streak of light that fell athwart her head and touched the white shoulder, the same dimpled hands, lightly folded, and the same rosy muslins blowing in the wind, that revealed glimpses of the same delicate foot just outlined in the picture.

I was so startled by her abrupt appearance, her strange laughter, and my own contending emotions, that all my wonted composure forsook me, and not one of the smooth speeches prepared for the interview came to my lips.

Bowing silently, I stood like an awkward lout till she completed my confusion by advancing with outstretched hand, saying, in a deliciously cordial tone:

"Welcome, cousin; your little plot was well laid; but a woman is hard to deceive, especially when such a tell-tale face as yours tries to put on a mask."

As she spoke she pointed to a mirror which reflected both my own figure and that of a gay and gallant ancestor, whose handsome face showed the most marked features of our race. I saw the likeness at once, for my mustache, curling hair, and velvet paletot added to the effect most strikingly.

Something in the compliment, as well as her own frank air, restored my self-possession, and, eager to remove all recollection of my *gaucherie,* I joined in her laughter, saying, gayly, as I kissed her hand with the Italian devotion that women like:

"A thousand pardons for attempting to deceive these bright eyes; but the banished prince longed to see the new queen, and so ventured home in disguise."

"I forgive the ruse, because you say *home* in a tone that betrays in you the same solitude that I feel. It is a large, lonely house. There is room enough for both, and as we are the last of our race, why not cease to be strangers and both come home?"

Nothing could have been more sweet and simple than look, voice and manner as she said this. It touched me, and yet the vague feeling of distrust born of my scrutiny of both the painted and living face still lingered in my mind, and robbed my answer of the warmth it should have possessed.

"Miss Stanhope forgets that I have lost my right to take shelter here. But since I have seen her my disappointment is much softened, because for a woman young and beautiful it would be far harder to work for bread than for a man whose bosom friends for years have been poverty and solitude."

She looked at me with a sudden dew in those proud eyes of hers, and for a moment stood silent, with the color varying in her cheeks; then, as if obeying a generous impulse, she smiled, and looking up at me, said, in a tone whose persuasive gentleness was irresistible:

"Cousin Cecil, promise to stay one week, and learn to know me better. I ask it as a favor; and since you possess the Stanhope pride, you shall make me your debtor by finishing this picture. The artist who began it will not return; for his own sake I forbid it."

A disdainful little gesture told the story of the cause of this banishment as plainly as words, and was, perhaps, a warning hint to me. I smiled at it, even while I felt as the fisher might have done when the Lorelei first began to charm him.

"I will stay," I briefly said, and then she asked me about my life in Italy, so pleasantly beguiling confidence after confidence from me, that if I had possessed a secret it would inevitably have passed into her keeping.

I staid, and day after day we sat in the long gallery, surrounded by beauty of all kinds, talking with ever-increasing frankness, while I painted this lovely cousin, who bewildered my senses without touching my heart.

The old lady who played duenna left us free, and little company disturbed the charming solitude that never lost its delight to me.

A whim had seized Cecelia to change the costume in the portrait from modern to ancient, and as the dress of a beautiful ancestress was still preserved, she put it on, enhancing her beauty fourfold by the rich brocades, the antique jewels, and priceless laces of past days.

"This little shoe must have a buckle if it is to be visible, as I beg it may be," I said, as she came rustling in one morning like a *grande dame* of the olden time.

"Bring the steel-bound casket, Adele; we may find something there that will suit this masquerade," said Cecelia to the maid who held her train.

Slipping off the coquettish shoe of white silk with a scarlet heel, she let me amuse myself with trying which of many ornaments would suit it best, while she absently clasped and unclasped the bracelets on her round arm.

"This is in perfect taste, and a picture in itself," I presently exclaimed, holding up the little shoe ornamented with a great buckle of chased silver, set here and there with a diamond, and a true-lover knot formed of a double S in the middle.

"That is one of the very buckles our gallant ancestor wore. You can see them in the picture yonder, and the story goes that they were given him by his lady-love," answered Cecelia, pointing to the portrait of Sir Sidney Stanhope hanging behind us.

This little fact led me to examine the trinkets with interest, and having put it into the silken shoe, I fell to painting it, while my lovely sitter amused me with old legends of our family.

The week had lengthened to three, and I still lingered, for it was evident that my cousin, with a woman's generosity, was willing to make the only reparation in her power. I felt sure that the idea came to her that first day, when, after the long pause, she bade me stay, with varying color and wet eyes betraying pity, interest, and the dawning affection of a lonely heart quick to feel the ties of family. I tried to love her, and grew feverish in my efforts to discover why, in spite of the fascination of her presence, I could not yield my heart wholly to her power. What cause had I to distrust this beautiful and generous girl? None; and yet I did, so much so that I found myself watching her with a curious persistence, as if some subtle instinct warned me to beware.

This habit, and the restlessness which possessed me, led me to roam about the house and grounds by night when all was quiet. My out-of-door life in Italy made this freedom necessary to me, and I indulged my whim so skillfully that no one but the watchdogs suspected it—they knew me, and kept my secret.

One evening twilight overtook me at my easel, and the summons to dinner left Cecelia no time to change her dress. Laughing at the strange contrast between our costumes, I led her to the table, and as I watched the brilliant figure opposite me, I revolved to know my fate that night, and if I had deceived myself, to break away at once from the spell that was increasing daily.

As soon as we were alone again, I led her out along the terrace, and as we paced there, arm-in-arm, I told her my hope and waited for her reply. A strange expression of relief dawned in her face as she looked up at me with eyes full of a tender melancholy.

"I hoped you would tell me this. Do not think it unmaidenly, but believe that I saw no other way of sharing this good fortune with you," she said in a voice curiously calm for such confessions.

"But, dear, I will have no sacrifice for me. If you love me, I accept the rest; otherwise not a penny will I touch," I said, decidedly, for her manner disturbed me.

"*If* I love you!" she cried; "how could I help it when you are all I have in the wide world to keep me from ———"

There she caught back some word that trembled on her lips, and threw herself into my arms, weeping passionately.

Annoyed, yet touched, I soothed her, hoping to receive some explanation of this sudden outburst, which seemed more like remorseful grief than happy love. But quickly recovering herself, she murmured, brokenly:

"I have been so alone all my life—exiled from home, I knew not why—kept in ignorance of parents and friends till all were gone—my youth has been so sad that happiness overcomes me."

Here her little maid came to deliver a note; Cecelia stepped into the stream of light which lay across the terrace from the long, open window of the drawing-room, read a few lines that seemed scrawled on a rough bit of paper, told Adele to say she would come to-morrow, and tearing the note to atoms, she rejoined me, saying, carelessly:

"A message from Elspeth, my old nurse, who is ill, and sends for me."

I thought nothing of the note, but why did her heart beat so fast as I drew her to me again? Why were her eyes so absent, her face so full of mingled anger, fear and contempt? and why did she shiver as if, to her, the sultry summer night had suddenly grown cold? But when I asked what troubled her, she shyly said she was agitated by happiness alone, then led me in and sang delightfully till bedtime. As we parted for the night she fixed her eyes on me with a strangely tragic look, and whispered in her sweetest tone:

"Sleep well, Cecil, and be sure I love you."

I went to my room, but did not sleep at all, for my thoughts worried me, and as soon as the house was still I stepped out of my window and roamed away into the park. A storm was gathering, and black clouds swept across the moon, making fitful light and shade; a hot wind blew strongly, and flashes of lightning darted from the gloomy west. The unquiet night suited my mood, and I wandered on, lost in my own thoughts, till a peal of thunder roused me. Looking about for shelter, as I was now a long way from the hall, I saw a steady gleam not far distant, and making my way to the bottom of a wild glen, I found a little hovel half hidden among the trees.

Peering in at the low window before I asked admittance, I saw, by the dim light of one candle, an old crone sitting on the hearth, her withered face turned attentively toward another figure which stood nearer the door—a woman, evidently, though so shrouded in a cloak that age or sex was hard to guess. Her back was turned toward me, her voice fierce and low, her attitude one of command, and the words she uttered so peculiar that they arrested my attention at once.

"If you dare to speak or show yourself till I give you leave, I will silence you in the surest way. I fear nothing, and having played the perilous game so far, I will not be robbed of success when it is dearest, by the threats of a helpless old woman."

"Not so helpless as you think, ungrateful girl; feeble, old, and forgotten as I am, I can undo what I have done by a word, and I will, I swear, if you are not kinder," cried the old woman in a shrill, angry voice. "You promised I should stay with you, should have every care and comfort, and receive a generous share of all you got; but now you keep me here in this unwholesome place, with no one to speak to but half-witted Kate; you never come till I scare you into obedience, and you give me nothing but a paltry pound now and then. You know I'm too lame to escape, and you threaten me if I complain; but hark you, my lady, I set you up and I can pull you down whether you murder me or not, for it's all on paper, safe hidden from you, but sure to come to light if anything goes wrong with me."

As the old woman paused, breathless with her wrath and exultation, the younger stamped her foot with uncontrollable impatience, and clinched the slender white hand that was visible, but her next words were kinder, though bitter contempt lurked in her tone.

"You may trust me, grandmother; I'll not harm you unless you rouse the mad temper which I cannot control. You know why I do not take you home till my own place is secure. You are old, you forget, and babble of things safer untold. Here, it can make no trouble for either of us, but with me, surrounded by curious servants, mischief would come to both. Can you not wait a little longer, and remember that in undoing me you as surely ruin yourself, since you are the greater criminal."

"It would go hard with both of us, but my age would serve me better than your beauty, for I can be humble, but you have the pride of a devil, and death itself could not bend it. I'll wait, but I must have money, my fair share; I like to see and touch it, to make sure of it, for you may deceive me as you do the world, and slip away, leaving me to pay the penalty while you enjoy the pleasure."

"You shall have it as soon as I can get it without exciting suspicion by the demand. An opportunity will soon come, and I will not forget you."

"You mean this marriage?"

"Yes."

"Then you will really do it?"

"I will, for I love him."

"Good! that makes all safe. Now go, child, before the storm breaks, but come often, or I will send for you, and if there is any sign of false play my story goes to this man, and I'll buy my own safety by betraying you."

"Agreed. Good-night," and the shrouded figure was gone like a shadow.

I meant to follow it, led by an uncontrollable impulse, but as I paused to let her gain a safe distance, the movements of the old woman arrested me. Nodding and mumbling with weird intelligence, she lifted one of the flat hearthstones and drew out a packet of papers, over which she seemed to gloat, muttering, as she peered at the scrawled pages:

"I'm old, but I'm wary, and not to be shaken off till I get my share of plunder. She thinks to scare me, but Kate knows where to find my secret if anything goes wrong with me. I've tutored her, and my lady will be outwitted at the last."

Chuckling, the old crone put her treasure back, and, raking up the fire, hobbled away to bed. I waited till her light was out, resolving to secure those papers, for I could not divest myself of the conviction that this secret concerned me. I had not caught a glimpse of the younger woman's face, the voice was unknown, the figure hidden, and the white hand might have belonged to any lady, yet I felt a strong suspicion that this mysterious woman was Cecelia, and this evil-minded beldame was old Elspeth.

The storm broke, but I did not heed it, for my new purpose absorbed me. As soon as all was still I gently forced the low lattice, stepped in, and groping my way to the hearth, stirred the smoldering embers till a little blaze shot up, showing me the flat stone, and glittering also on an object that brought confirmation to my dark suspicions, for there, where the unknown girl had stood, lay the silver buckle. I caught it up, examined it by the dim light, and could not doubt my own eyes; it was Sir Sidney's antique ornament, and that impatient gesture of Cecelia's foot had left it here to betray her. I could readily understand how in her eagerness to slip away she had hastily changed the brocades for a simpler dress, forgetting to remove the shoes. Now I was sure of my right to seize the papers, and having done so stole noiselessly away.

Till dawn the storm raged furiously, and till dawn I sat in my room reading, thinking and resolving, for those badly-written pages showed me that the future I had pictured to myself never could be mine. The charm was broken, the warning instinct justified, and an impassable gulf opened between my cousin and myself. As the sun rose my plan was laid, and making a careful toilet, I tried to remove from my face, also, all trace of that night's experience, but did not entirely succeed, for the glass showed me a pale cheek, eyes full of a gloomy fire, and lips sternly set.

I often breakfasted alone, for Cecelia kept luxurious hours, and we seldom met till noon. That day I waited impatiently in the gallery where we had agreed to have a last sitting. My impatience did me good service, however, for when at last she came my paleness was replaced by a feverish warmth, and the stern lips had been trained to meet her with a smile.

"Good-morning, Cecil," she said, with an enchanting glance and a conscious blush as she gave me her hand.

I did not kiss it as usual, but holding it loosely I examined the soft little fingers outstretched in my palm, wondering as I did so if they could be the same I last night saw so fiercely clinched.

"What is it?" she asked, looking up at me with playful wonder in the eyes now grown so soft.

"Perhaps I was thinking of the ring that should be here," I

answered, feeling a curious desire to test the love of this un-happy girl.

"I never thought I should consent to wear even so small a fetter as a wedding-ring, I love my liberty so well; but if you put it on it will not burden me, for you will be a tender and a generous master, Cecil," she answered, turning toward her accustomed seat to hide the emotion she was too proud to show me.

"I have the faults of my race—an unbending will, an unfor-giving spirit, and 'the pride of a devil,' so beware, cousin."

She started as I quoted the old woman's phrase and shot a quick glance at me, but I was tranquilly preparing my palette, and she sat down with a relieved, yet weary air.

"Could you be as unmerciful as old Sir Guy, who cursed his only child for deceiving him?" she asked, lifting her eyes to the portrait of a stern-faced cavalier hanging next to debonnair Sir Sidney.

"I could, for treachery turns my heart to stone."

I saw a slight shiver pass over her, and leaning her head on her hand she sat silent while I touched up a jewel here, a silken fold there, or added a brighter gold to the beautiful hair. She looked fair, young and tender, but, as I had said, treachery turned my heart to stone, and I did not spare her.

"You are *triste* to-day, sweetheart; let me amuse you as you have often done me by a legend of our family. I lately found it in an old manuscript which I will show you by-and-by."

"Thanks; I like old stories if they are strong and tragic," she answered, with a smile, as she lay back in the great chair in an attitude of luxurious indolence.

"Why, you have forgotten the little shoe; I meant to touch up the brilliant buckle and add a deeper scarlet to the coquett-ish heel. Shall I bid Adele bring it?" I asked, looking from the black satin slipper to the tranquil face lying on the purple cushion.

"No, it hurt my foot and I threw it away in a pet," she answered, with a little frown.

"Not buckle and all I hope, that is an heirloom."

"I have it safe, but the painted one is so well done I will not have it touched. Let my eyes outshine my jewels, as you gallantly averred they did, and tell your tale while you paint, for I am sadly indolent to-day."

As she added falsehood to falsehood, my heart beat indignantly against the traitorous ornament safely hidden in my breast, but my face did not betray me, and I obeyed her, glancing up from time to time to mark the effect of my words, not that of my work, for I painted with a colorless brush.

"Sir Marmaduke, for whom our uncle was named, I fancy, was a stern man who married late, and treated his wife so ill that she left him, taking with her their little child, for, being a girl, the old man had no love for it. Both the poor things died in a foreign land, and Sidney yonder, the comely nephew, was the lawful heir to the estate. The last words of the old man seemed to express his wish that it should be so, and the nephew was about to claim his own when the daughter reappeared and proved her right to the fortune. You are pale, love—does my dull story weary you?"

"No, it is only the heat. Go on, I listen," and half hiding the tell-tale cheek with her hand, she sat with downcast eyes, and a face that slowly grew a colorless mask with the effort to subdue emotion.

"The old manuscript is not very clear on this point; but I gather that the neglected girl's reported death was only a ruse to shield her from her cruel father. Her claim was accepted, and poor Sidney left to poverty again. Now comes the romance of the tale. He went to see this new-found cousin; she was beautiful and gracious, seemed eager to share her prize, and generously offered the young man a home. This touched and won him. She soon evidently loved him, and in spite of an inward distrust, he *fancied* he returned the passion."

As I slightly emphasized a word here and there in that last sentence, a fiery glow spread over that white face from neck to brow, the haughty eyes flashed full upon me, and the red lips trembled as if passionate words were with difficulty restrained. I saw that my shaft told, and with resentful coolness I went on, still preserving the gay, light tone that made the truth doubly bitter and taunting.

"Take the fan that lies in your lap, dearest; this heat oppresses you. Yes, it was very curious to read how this lover was fascinated in spite of himself, and how he fought against his doubts till he tried to put an end to them by asking the hand extended to him."

The dimpled hand lying on the arm of the chair was clinched suddenly, and I saw again the hand of the cloaked woman in the wood, and smiling to myself at this new confirmation, I continued:

"But here begins the tragedy which you like so well. The cousins were betrothed, and that very night Sidney, who was given to late wanderings, went out to dream lover's dreams, in spite of a gathering storm which drove him for shelter to a little cottage in the wood. Here he overheard a strange conversation between an old creature and a mysterious woman whose face he could not see." (How her eyes glittered as she listened! and what a long breath of relief escaped her at those last words!) "This lively gossip excited Sidney's curiosity, and when the lady vanished, leaving this traitor behind her" (here I produced the buckle), "this bold young man, guided by the mutterings of the crone, found and secured a strange confession of the treachery of both."

Here Cecelia rose erect in her chair, and from that moment her eyes never left my face as she listened, still and colorless as the statue behind her. I think any sign of weakness or remorse would have touched me even then, but she showed none, and her indomitable pride roused mine, making me pitiless. Brush and palette lay idle now, and looking straight at the fair, false face before me, I rapidly ended the story which I had begun in the disguise of an ancient legend.

"It seems that the old woman had been the confidential servant of Sir Marmaduke's wife, and had a grudge of her own against her master. When my lady and the child died, for die they did, as reported, this woman bided her time, artfully securing letters, tokens, and other proofs, to use when the hour came. At Sir Marmaduke's death she put forward her grandchild, the natural daughter of the old man, inheriting both the beauty and the spirit of her race. This girl played her part well; the plot succeeded, and if the sordid nature of the granddame had not irritated the heiress and kept her in danger of discovery, all would have worked admirably. Half justice, under the guise of generosity, soothed whatever pangs of remorse the girl felt, and as she loved Sidney, she believed that she could expiate the wrong she did him by keeping him happily blind to the treachery of a wife he trusted. A terrible mistake, for when he discovered this deceit, the old distrust turned to contempt, gratitude to wrath, and love to loathing."

"What did he do?" she whispered, with white lips, as an agony of shame, despair, and love looked at me from the tragic eyes.

"I had risen and looked down at her with an uncontrollable pity softening my stern face."

"Possessing something of the chivalry of his race, he disdained to crush her even by one reproach; but though forced to decline the proposed alliance, he freely offered her safety and a maintenance, never forgetting that, in spite of deceit, and sin, and shame, she was a woman and his cousin."

"Did he think she would accept?" she cried, lifting the head that had sunk lower and lower as I spoke till all the warm-hued hair swept to her feet.

I had risen and looked down at her with an uncontrollable pity softening my stern face. I answered briefly:

"Yes, for where else could she find help but at the hands of her kinsman?"

She sprang up, as if my compassion was more bitter to hear than my contempt, the fiery spirit rebelled against me, and love itself yielded to the pride that ruled her.

"Not even the offer of a favor will I accept from you, for I have a kinder friend to fly to. Take your rightful place, and enjoy it if you can, haunted as it must be by the memory of the stain I have brought upon the name you are so proud of."

She hurried, as if to leave me, but pausing at the easel, cast a sudden look at the smiling image of herself, and as if anxious to leave no trace behind, she caught up my palette-knife, scored the canvas up and down till it hung in strips; then with a laugh which echoed long in my ears she swept slowly down the long gallery, passed through the wide window at the further end to the balcony that overhung the court below, and standing there with the sunshine streaming over her, she looked back at me with an expression which fixed that moment in my memory for ever.

Like a brilliant picture, she stood there with the light full on her shining hair, jeweled arms, rich robes, and stately form, all contrasting sharply with the wild and woeful face looking backward with a mute farewell.

On that instant a terrible foreboding of her purpose flashed over me, and I rushed forward to restrain her; but too late, for with a wave of the white hand she was gone.

Death was the kinder friend to whom she had flown, and when I found her in the courtyard, shattered by that cruel fall, she smiled the old proud smile, and put away the hand that would have lifted her so tenderly.

"Let me die here; I have no other home," she whispered, faintly; then her face softened as she looked up at my pallid face, and feebly trying to fold her hands, she murmured, tenderly:

"Forgive me, for I loved you!"

Those were her last words, and as they passed her lips, I saw nothing but a beautiful dead woman lying at my feet, and Sir Sidney's diamond buckle glittering in the sun, as it fell from my breast to receive a bloody stain which lingers still on that relic of my unhappy cousin.

La Belle Bayadère

Chapter I

THE WHOLE OF THE IMMENSE STAGE represented a tropical forest, with the skillful fidelity which French artists bring to such work. A wide river, starred with lotus flowers, flowed through the luxuriant jungle; moonlight filled the green gloom with mellow radiance, and unseen music lent enchantment to the delicious solitude. Before the first sound of applause could express the satisfaction of the brilliant audience, stealthy steps seemed to come creeping through the wood, and just when expectation was at its height, a magnificent tiger bounded from the jungle and vanished in its lair. It was a real tiger, and this daring surprise charmed the excitable Parisians by its very danger.

The well-trained beast's *début* was hailed by loud applause, for the chains it wore were invisible, and the wild scene seemed wonderfully real.

"How well it opens! Even you, my *blasé* Philip, will become enthusiastic, I think, as the piece goes on," said beautiful Mrs. Cope, turning toward her husband—a handsome, indolent-looking man, who lounged beside her with an air of supreme indifference to all about him.

"I doubt it, Maud, but if anything could stir me up a trifle it would be these souvenirs of India," he replied, gently yawning behind his hand.

"I thought so, and for that reason persuaded you to come. You want a new sensation, an excitement of some sort, and I promised to give you one. In a few minutes, I suspect, you will own that I have kept my word," and the tender eyes of the young wife turned half-wistfully, half-triumphantly to the dark face of her listless husband.

"I will welcome anything that shall put fire, spice, and interest into my life here in this tame country; but I fancy your idea of excitement, my friend, differs from mine as much as a tiger-hunt does from a flower-show."

Before Mrs. Cope could reply, a sudden change in the music announced the arrival of the hero of the piece. With the barbaric clash of cymbal, drum and horn, the splendors of a mounted guard, and all the pomp of an Eastern satrap, Prince Acbar appeared, reclining on a scarlet and gold howda borne by a white elephant—a slender, swarthy young Indian with magnificent eyes and figure, who looked his part to the life, and played it with spirit, rapidly alternating from the graceful languor to the fiery activity of a true Oriental.

"This is not bad, upon my word," said Cope, lifting his glass to examine the prince as he descended, stepping carelessly on the bowed backs of his kneeling slaves.

"Wait till you see the mate of this splendid creature. My sensation is yet to come," whispered Maud, with a smile.

A wild hunting-song from the guard, and a little necessary by-play, informed the audience that the prince was on a tiger-hunt, and having missed the beast after a long chase, was about to repose. Slaves arranged a luxurious couch of skins beside the river, and then, at an imperious wave of the master's hand, the train vanished, leaving the young man to drop asleep, lulled by the murmur of the stream.

A most effective tableau was produced by the handsome, brilliantly-appareled youth lying on his savage couch in an attitude of graceful abandon, with eyes dreamily fixed on the gleaming water, while behind him from the gloom of the cave glared the tiger's fierce head, stealthily appearing and disappearing as the treacherous brute prepared to spring upon its prey.

A stir of excitement filled the house, and glances of mingled fear and admiration were concentrated upon the daring beast-tamer as he lay tranquilly within reach of the royal tiger; but, as if to whet interest by delay, again the music changed, and a delicious melody entranced the ear.

A light mist floated down the river, and when it lifted, one of the magnified lotus flowers was seen to be unfolding. Leaf by leaf it spread till the last white petal fell, disclosing the "Spirit of the Ganges" nestling in its golden heart.

A diaphanous cloud of illusion revealed a little foot, a snowy arm, and a face of marvelous beauty, framed in waves of darkest hair, out of which shone lustrous eyes, full of a mysterious power.

The great golden showers seemed to surround this charming figure with a soft radiance as she rose, and leaving her flowery bed, danced over the moonlit water like a spirit of the summer night. It was a wonderful piece of art, for the airy grace of the rosy feet, the eloquent gestures of the lovely arms, the languid undulations of the exquisite figure, were beyond the skill of any known danseuse.

No effort was visible, no theatrical tinsel, no hackneyed step or pose marred the illusion, and the "poetry of motion" seemed perfectly illustrated as this strange girl, still half enveloped in the fleecy cloud, hovered to and fro before the entranced spectators.

Floating toward the shore along a path of light, she seemed to smile upon the prince as she sang a canzonet in a voice as full of passionate sweetness as her face was of subtle Southern beauty. In the song was given the key to the piece; the spirit tells her love for the mortal, and promises him the eternal joys of a Hindoo heaven if he is true to her.

As the last note died, the prince awoke from his dream and rushed forward as if to detain the lovely phantom; but like a wraith, she vanished, leaving only the white cloud in his eager arms.

At this instant the tiger leaped, and the young man, rudely startled from his trance, uttered so natural a cry of alarm that many involuntarily echoed it. Then followed the fight which was the *chef-d'œuvre* of this remarkable beast-tamer.

The well-trained animal played its part so perfectly that women turned pale and men breathed hard as they watched man and monster wrestling together, in such seeming deadly earnest that for a time nothing was visible but a mass of tawny fur, supple brown limbs, savage eyes, and the flash of jeweled robes.

The man came uppermost at last, and clutching the brute by the throat, knelt on its panting breast as he apparently drove his dagger into its vitals with a cry of exultation. A brief struggle, a faint attempt to rend its victor, and the tiger rolled lifeless at the feet of the prince, whom the excited spectators overwhelmed with acclamations.

As the curtain fell, Mrs. Cope drew a long breath of relief, and glanced at her husband to see if he showed any sign of interest yet. She was satisfied—nay, even startled by the entire change which had passed over him.

He sat erect, with wide open eyes, lips apart, and the air of one who had been suddenly surprised out of himself. More than this, his bronzed cheek was pale, his hand clutched the cushioned rail with unconscious vehemence, and he stared at the green curtain before him, as if on its blank surface he saw some figure which absorbed his thoughts.

"What is it, Philip? You look as if you had seen a ghost," whispered his wife, amazed at his appearance.

"I have!" he answered, without stirring.

"Was it the fight that excites you so strangely?"

"I scarcely saw it."

"Then it is the 'Spirit of the Ganges,' and my test succeeds."

"Who is she?" and Cope drew his hand across his face, as to compose his features to their wonted calm.

"I know nothing of her, except that she is the last new sensation. A Spaniard, some one said, and destined to take Paris by storm."

"No Spaniard ever danced like that. I have often tried to describe the Eastern Bayadères—now you have seen one."

"How do you know?"

"No other dancers use the arms more than the feet, or have the art to make each gesture express an emotion. No other women are so lovely, or possess the power of making their beauty felt."

"You speak warmly, and you should know," answered Mrs. Cope, with a troubled look. "This charming creature certainly got herself up wonderfully for the part, and played like a born sprite."

"Better even than you think, for none but a true Hindoo would have remembered the *khol* on the eyelids, the *henna* on the finger-tips, the gauzy *tab* over the bosom, or worn bangles with such ease, and dared attempt to dance with bare feet. Yes, she *is* beautiful, this unknown, who is to enslave all Paris as she has me!"

A strange expression of mingled exultation and melancholy passed over the man's face as he spoke, and turning from his wife, he fell to studying the hitherto neglected playbill, as if eager to gather some intelligence from it.

"What have I done?" cried the poor woman, within herself. "I hoped to amuse him for an hour, and perhaps I have lost him for ever. I tried to banish ennui, and have kindled a flame that may consume my peace. These souvenirs of India recall something more tender than tiger-hunts, and these handsome Indians transport him to the land where, perhaps, the romance of his youth was known."

Here the curtain rose again; but now Cope was the breathless spectator, and his wife, forgetting her interest in the play, watched him keenly, feeling that the test she innocently applied possessed a power she had not suspected.

The scenes which followed were all unusually brilliant, piquant, or daring. La Belle Bayadère danced but three times, yet she created a furore at each appearance, for her beauty, grace and style were too new and striking to fail of impressing the novelty-mad Parisians with the wildest admiration.

Her second dance was in the harem of the prince, who is endeavoring to forget his haunting dream of the "Spirit," in the charms of a bevy of Georgian slaves whom a merchant exhibits. One by one the fair girls sang and danced before him, but all failed to please till Mademoiselle Rahel, the pet danseuse of Paris, executed her most famous *pas* in her best manner. The audience greeted her with enthusiasm, the prince smiled upon her, and the panting beauty was about to accept the royal favor extended to her, when, with startling abruptness, the music broke into a wild strain, and out from the central fountain flashed La Belle Bayadère like a flame of fire.

Scarlet, white and gold was her dress, silver bangles shone on slender wrist and ankle, fire-flies seemed imprisoned in her dusky hair, and she kept time to her winged steps with the clash of cymbals as she danced as no woman had ever danced on that stage before. She seemed another creature from the airy sylph of the moonlight river. All now was fire and force, no leap too daring, no step too intricate, no pose impossible to the agile grace of the lithe figure which darted to and fro like a wandering flame. The vivid coloring, intense vitality, and marvelous skill of the creature electrified actors and audience; all followed her with dazzled eyes, completely carried away by the spirit of that amazing dance. Louder and louder rose the music, faster and faster flew the little feet, wilder and wilder grew the frenzy which seemed to possess the girl, till nothing was visible but a brilliant maze of scarlet drapery, flying hair, and a face inspired by something far more potent than a spirit of rivalry. Then, at the very acme of this enchanting abandon, the music snapped in a broken chord, and with a single ringing clash of the cymbals, the Bayadère paused as if turned to stone, stood for one instant radiant and regal, in an attitude of indescribable grace, and vanished as swiftly as she came.

Before the curtain was fairly down, Cope had darted from the box with a face as full of energy and fire as that of the mimic prince who had watched the beautiful dancer with the pride and ardor of a real lover. Mrs. Cope hid herself behind the curtains of her box, agitated with conflicting hopes and fears, for every moment confirmed her suspicion that she had unwittingly touched some secret sin or sorrow of her husband's past. Not till the last bell rang, after an unusually long pause, did he reappear, flushed, breathless and excited, bringing with him a singular bouquet, formed entirely of cactus-blossoms of the most vivid scarlet, surmounted by their own prickly leaves.

"For whom is that savage-looking nosegay, Philip?" asked Mrs. Cope, as he threw himself into a chair and fixed his eyes eagerly on the ascending curtain.

"Wait and see, madame," he briefly answered in the imperious tone she had often resented for the sake of others, yet never heard addressed to herself before.

She was a proud woman, and his manner wounded her deeply. She set her lips, and her eyes kindled as she said, in a cool, significant tone which arrested his attention in spite of himself:

"I will; and when you fling your thorny gift to the girl, I will offer my roses to her handsome husband."

"Her what?" and Cope turned on her a quick glance full of doubt and dismay.

"I have been told that the young pair are newly married, and fancy it is true, for they play like lovers."

"A jealous woman's fancy," and he looked away with an incredulous shrug.

"Watch and see," she said, echoing his tone if not his words exactly.

"I will!" and Cope's face wore an ominous smile as he turned to follow the handsome Indian through several scenes, in which he and his beasts played stirring parts. Not till the closing act did the charming girl reappear and give an intense interest to a spectacle which one observer watched with an almost fierce scrutiny. As a grand finale the prince is cast into a den of wild beasts by his enemies, to whom he has been treacherously betrayed, and the last scene displayed the faithful lover in a gloomy amphitheatre, surrounded by foes above and savage brutes below. One tiger lay as if already slain by the hero, who waits, wounded but undismayed, the attack of a still more formidable assailant. All the animals were safely held by artfully-hidden chains, except the lion, who was about to destroy the much-enduring prince. He looked a magnificent brute as he stood surveying his victim with thunderous growls, but he was old, toothless, heavily drugged, and his master's all-powerful eye never left him a moment; therefore the danger was slight, great as it appeared. Many shuddered as they looked, and some cried out as the lion crouched before he sprung, but at the instant the dancer bounded over the iron bars which surrounded the mimic amphitheatre, and alighted just between the brute and his prey.

"Great heavens, what courage!" exclaimed the spell-bound audience, as the dauntless creature warily approached the lion, who retreated as she advanced. Half way round the enclosure she paused, and with a rapid gesture flung a golden chain about the royal beast, who dropped submissively at her feet, as if the light fetter possessed an irresistible power. Dancing airily to and fro among the animals, she seemed to cast a spell on all, for one by one they shrunk and cowered before the little red-tipped wand she carried, for the painted toy was as potent in their eyes as the red-hot iron rod their master used to train and conquer them with. As the last leopard fawned at her feet the girl executed a joyful *pas seul* as wonderful as the others had been, and at the end threw herself into the arms of the prince, signifying that the reward was won. A gorgeous transformation scene closed the spectacle with the splendors of a Hindoo paradise, whither the lovers are welcomed by houris to a life of eternal delight.

"She must come now. She dare not refuse to accept our homage," was the universal exclamation as a frantic encore thundered through the house, assuring the unknown danseuse that fame and fortune were awaiting her. "The Spirit of the Ganges" was pronounced a grand success.

She did come, but, as if bent on charming them entirely by her daring freaks, she led the captive lion with her, and while the comely actor gathered up the floral trophies that strewed the stage, she leaned against the stately brute with a nonchalant grace infinitely more effective than the most coquettish smiles or grateful obeisances.

Mrs. Cope forgot to fling her flowers, but Philip, leaning far over the box, cast his exactly at the girl's feet. She glanced up, and the proud weariness of her face flashed into sudden scorn and detestation as her great black eyes rested for an instant on the flushed, dark countenance bent toward her. Then, in the drawing of a breath, she set her foot upon the flowers with a gesture of disdain, and turning, gave her hand to the young Indian, wearing a smile of such tender meaning that few doubted the existence of a real romance behind the mimic one.

As they vanished Cope struck his clinched hand on the cushion before him, exclaiming in a vehement whisper:

"By heavens it *is* she!"

"Who? Oh, Philip, what have I done?" cried his wife, detaining him as he seemed about to go, forgetful of her presence.

He laughed a strange laugh, drew her hand under his arm as if recollecting himself, and said, abruptly:

"You have been trying to rouse me, as you call it, ever since we were married; rest satisfied, you have done it now with a vengeance."

Chapter II

FOR SIX WEEKS "The Spirit of the Ganges" was played nightly to packed houses; for six weeks Philip Cope made unavailing efforts to obtain an interview with the lovely danseuse, and for six weary weeks his wife watched him with the jealous vigilance of a proud and loving woman suddenly wakened from a brief dream of confidence and tenderness. She had "roused him with a vengeance," for, from the night when her entreaties had lured him to the theatre, he was an altered man. Brusque and cold, restless and absorbed, he seemed utterly unlike the lover who, with languid devotion, had wooed and won the girl who gladly gave her heart, refusing to believe that he sought her for her fortune, or the husband who for three months had been slowly falling back into the supreme indifference of a man who cared for nothing but his selfish ease. Now Maud began to believe that the elegant ennui was but a mask to cover some secret care, remorse or fear, and this sudden change from perfect indolence to sleepless energy perplexed and afflicted her.

Too proud to demand explanations which had been sternly refused to tender entreaties, she hid her doubts and fears under a calm front, and watched with untiring patience.

Night after night the two sat in their box silent but alert; day after day Philip besieged the dancer with notes and messages beseeching one word with her, and day and night the evil spell which had been cast over both worked its changes unsuspected by all but the subtle mind that gave it birth.

La Belle Bayadère became the rage in Paris, and added to her *éclat* the charm of mystery, for only on the stage was she visible to her adorers. When the curtain fell she vanished with her lover, and the most persistent curiosity could only discover that the Indian troupe lived secluded in a hotel which was reported to be a miracle of Eastern luxury. Surrounded by her own servants, faithful, silent and brave, the girl was inaccessible, and as she was never seen in public unaccompanied by Indra, the actor, it was in vain to attempt an interview till she willed it.

What Cope suffered in those weeks was but a foretaste of the years to come, and some dim consciousness of this may have given added bitterness to the long suspense, the keen regret, the vivid memories, and the hopeless desires which made that time a torment.

The announcement of the farewell representation of the favorite spectacle brought dismay to Cope and relief to his wife, who had discovered only that Philip had not met the dancer in spite of his unceasing efforts.

On the evening of that day, as Maud went to dress for the theatre, she found a tiny note on her toilet-table containing these words, written in a woman's hand:

"If you desire to know your husband's secret, follow without fear the messenger who will come for you at midnight."

"I will go," she said, with a resolute air, as she hid the billet in her bosom. "If it costs me my life I *will* know what Philip hides from me. Death cannot be worse than this suspense and doubt."

Suspecting whither she would be led, she made a grand toilet, feeling a woman's pride in heightening her beauty for a rival's eyes. As she swept into the *salon* she was joined by her husband, who, for some unknown reason, had made himself a marvel of elegance, and wore a look of triumph that caused the poor woman's heart to stand still with a nameless fear.

"For whom is all this splendor?" he asked, with a careless glance at the lovely wife before him.

"Not for you, Philip. You no longer care for the beauty you once praised. I dress to do honor to La Belle Bayadère," answered Maud, with a keen look.

"I, also," and he gave her back a smile that seemed to defy doubt, reproach and shame.

"Philip, have you nothing to tell me? I can forgive and forget much for your sake. I shall never ask again. Be just, be generous, and do not let a mystery estrange us."

As she spoke with a sudden impulse of tenderness, Maud stretched her hands imploringly toward him, hoping he would spare her from playing the spy by a frank confession. But the glamour of an old love was over him, truth and pity were not in him, and a daring hope had just been kindled which blinded him to right and justice. Hardening his heart, and steeling his face, he met her pathetic appeal with a mocking bow, and said:

"Your interest flatters me; but I have no interesting confidences to bestow. Permit me to button your gloves, for the carriage waits."

But the fingers that performed the little service trembled; as he led her down-stairs, Maud could hear his heart beat rapidly, and his face never lost the pale excitement, which was by turns exultant or intensely anxious.

Neither spoke again during the drive, and through the play an almost unbroken silence reigned in their box, for each was intent on some all-absorbing thought when the stage did not claim their entire attention.

Never had La Belle played more perfectly, and never had a farewell been more enthusiastic than that which she received when she smiled her adieu and was led away by the handsome Indra along a path carpeted with flowers.

"You will go home at once, of course. I have an engagement," said Cope, as he caught up his hat with ill-disguised impatience, and hurried his wife into the carriage.

"Good-night," she said, but he was gone, and she drove on with bitter tears dropping fast upon the hands locked fast together in her lap.

"Madame, it is I," said a low voice near her, and glancing up in alarm, she saw a venerable Indian seated opposite. "Have no fear. I am the messenger, and the time is nearly come," he said, in a reassuring tone; adding, gravely, "do you trust me?"

"Yes," she answered, trembling, yet resolved.

Without a word he leaned out, gave an order, and the carriage rolled rapidly in a new direction.

"Who sends for me?" she asked.

No answer but a finger on the lips, as the old man shook his head and sat motionless.

That night Cope had also received a message, for on his table he had found a single scarlet cactus and three words on a card beside it, "Come at twelve."

"At last—at last!" he had cried, seizing the flower and pressing the well-known signal to his lips. "I knew she would relent, and now nothing shall stand between us if she forgives."

This secret hope agitated him almost beyond control, and when at length free he hurried away to the long-desired interview. No guide was needed; he knew the way but too well, and paced to and fro before the hotel, waiting with fierce impatience for the appointed hour to strike.

As he stood in the courtyard a carriage dashed in, and a vailed lady descended and entered, accompanied by a venerable Indian.

"My Almèe!" murmured Cope, ardently, as he watched the shrouded figures vanish.

Ten minutes later the clocks struck, and he sprang up the steps, fearing no repulse now. Doors opened like magic before him, and he found himself in the long-desired presence of La Belle Bayadère.

Still in the costume she had worn as the "Spirit," the lovely woman looked lovelier than ever, for the flush of some strong emotion was on her cheek, its softness in her eyes, its tender music in her voice.

As Cope impetuously approached, she warned him back, saying, slowly, in the purest French:

"Not yet. I have much to say before I can embrace you. When you have confessed and done penance the reward may come."

"Almèe, forgive me! I will confess anything, do any penance to win my old place back. Say what you will, but do not keep me waiting long, for my patience has been hardly tried, and I am pining for my reward."

A strange smile passed over the girl's mobile features, but she only said:

"I, too, have waited, and now desire my reward. Listen, and tell me if this tale is not true. Two years ago, in India, an English soldier was wounded in a fight among the hills, left for dead by his men, and would have perished had not an old man, a Hindoo, befriended his enemy, taken him home, nursed and saved him. The Englishman feigned gratitude to the father and love to his daughter. They trusted him, and when he tired of them he betrayed the old man to death, and would have made the girl his slave, but she escaped."

"All true—God forgive me! but I did not feign love—I truly loved you, Almèe, and would have married you if it had been safe," broke in Cope, with mingled shame, remorse, and passion struggling in face and voice.

"Let that pass. The girl found a friend, and in time discovered the old lover whom she sought."

"Then, you have come to find me?" cried Cope, bewildered by the keen glitter of her eyes, the soft smile of her lips, and the measured tone of her clear voice.

"Yes, I searched for you through two long years, and found you at last more lost to me than when land and sea divided us."

"Faithful angel! Yes, in a desperate mood I sold myself for a woman's fortune. Till you came I found some pleasure in the bargain, spite of the burden attached, but now it is a worse slavery than the galleys. It has nearly maddened me since I beheld you again, and I'll break loose at once, for it will surely come to that sooner or later."

"You love me still?" asked Almèe, with a sudden tremor in her voice, as Cope paused, breathless and expectant.

"More passionately than ever, for absence has only made you fairer, remorse rendered you dearer, and companionship with a calm, cold Englishwoman shows me how infinitely sweeter is the ardent love, the deathless devotion of my Indian Almèe."

"Will you leave this stately wife, this hard-won wealth, your good name, and honorable place to win me—me, a dancing-girl, who have only my beauty for my dower?" asked the danseuse, bending on him that searching look, while her bosom heaved with the emotions she suppressed.

"I will, and you know it, for the old spirit woke when I saw you; the reckless courage, the wild nature, the fiery heart are all here, hidden so long only to break out stronger than before. Try me. For your sake I will defy the world, and fly to the desert again with my little queen."

Quite carried away by his own untameable desires, Cope threw himself at her feet, and waited her reply without fear. How her eyes shone with sudden fire, and her red lips curled with pride as she watched the man before her, utterly subjugated to her will in spite of all the obstacles that should have restrained him!

In the drawing of a breath her whole air changed, her face was full of the intensest scorn, and her voice startled him by its sharp, stern accent, as she said, with a slow, triumphant smile:

"I am satisfied! For this I have worked and waited; for this I have led you on to break every tie that should bind an honorable

"'In vain! Oh, Almèe, do not mock me! What stands between us now?' cried Cope, bewildered. 'My husband and your wife.' As the words fell from her lips, she pointed toward two curtained alcoves behind her."

man, to sacrifice all hope of future peace, and to find too late that it has been in vain."

"In vain! Oh, Almèe, do not mock me! What stands between us now?" cried Cope, bewildered.

"My husband and your wife."

As the words fell from her lips, she pointed toward two curtained alcoves behind her, and, as if obeying her gesture, the purple draperies parted, showing Indra, splendid in his youth, beauty, and happiness, and Maud, the pale ghost of her former self, while in her eyes burned the quenchless fire of a proud woman's resentment.

In the dead pause that followed, Cope felt to his heart's core the bitter sting of a shame which never could be effaced, owned that Almèe's subtle vengeance had wrecked his life, and followed his wife without a word, when La Belle Bayadère threw herself into Indra's arms, saying, briefly:

"Go! we want no shadow on our happiness."

Bibliography

This chronological listing contains all located Alcott thrillers.

"Marion Earle: or, Only an Actress!" *American Union* (ca. July–12 September 1858). Repr. in *New York Atlas* (12 September 1858).

"Pauline's Passion and Punishment," *Frank Leslie's Illustrated Newspaper* (3 and 10 January 1863). Repr. in *Behind a Mask: The Unknown Thrillers of Louisa May Alcott,* ed. Madeleine B. Stern (New York: William Morrow, 1975).

"A Whisper in the Dark," *Frank Leslie's Illustrated Newspaper* (6 and 13 June 1863). Repr. in *A Modern Mephistopheles and A Whisper in the Dark* (Boston: Roberts Brothers, 1889); and in *Plots and Counterplots: More Unknown Thrillers of Louisa May Alcott,* ed. Madeleine B. Stern (New York: William Morrow, 1976).

"A Pair of Eyes; or, Modern Magic," *Frank Leslie's Illustrated Newspaper* (24 and 31 October 1863). Repr. in *A Double Life: Newly Discovered Thrillers of Louisa May Alcott,* ed. Madeleine B. Stern, Joel Myerson, and Daniel Shealy (Boston: Little, Brown, 1988).

"Enigmas," *Frank Leslie's Illustrated Newspaper* (14 and 21 May 1864). Repr. in *Frank Leslie's Popular Monthly* (April 1876).

"V.V.; or, Plots and Counterplots," *The Flag of Our Union* (4, 11, 18, and 25 February 1865). Repr. as ten-cent novelette by A. M. Barnard (Boston: Thomes & Talbot, ca. 1870); and in *Plots and Counterplots,* ed. Madeleine B. Stern (New York: William Morrow, 1976).

"The Fate of the Forrests," *Frank Leslie's Illustrated Newspaper* (11, 18,

· 163 ·

and 25 February 1865). Repr. in *A Double Life,* ed. Madeleine B. Stern, Joel Myerson, and Daniel Shealy (Boston: Little, Brown, 1988).

"A Marble Woman: or, The Mysterious Model," *The Flag of Our Union* (20, 27 May and 3, 10 June 1865). Repr. in *Plots and Counterplots,* ed. Madeleine B. Stern (New York: William Morrow, 1976).

"A Double Tragedy. An Actor's Story," *Frank Leslie's Chimney Corner* (3 June 1865). Repr. in *A Double Life,* ed. Madeleine B. Stern, Joel Myerson, and Daniel Shealy (Boston: Little, Brown, 1988).

"Ariel. A Legend of the Lighthouse," *Frank Leslie's Chimney Corner* (8 and 15 July 1865). Repr. in *A Double Life,* ed. Madeleine B. Stern, Joel Myerson, and Daniel Shealy (Boston: Little, Brown, 1988).

"A Nurse's Story," *Frank Leslie's Chimney Corner* (2, 9, 16, 23, 30 December 1865 and 6 January 1866). Repr. in *Freaks of Genius: Unknown Thrillers of Louisa May Alcott,* ed. Daniel Shealy, Madeleine B. Stern, and Joel Myerson (Westport, Conn.: Greenwood, 1991).

"Behind a Mask: or, A Woman's Power," *The Flag of Our Union* (13, 20, 27 October and 3 November 1866). Repr. in *Behind a Mask,* ed. Madeleine B. Stern (New York: William Morrow, 1975).

"The Freak of a Genius," *Frank Leslie's Illustrated Newspaper* (20, 27 October and 3, 10, 17 November 1866). Repr. in *Freaks of Genius,* ed. Daniel Shealy, Madeleine B. Stern, and Joel Myerson (Westport, Conn.: Greenwood, 1991).

The Mysterious Key, and What It Opened (Boston: Elliott, Thomes & Talbot, [1867]). No. 50 in *Ten Cent Novelettes* series of *Standard American Authors.* Repr. as No. 382 in *The Leisure Hour Library* (New York: F. M. Lupton, ca. 1900); and in *Behind a Mask,* ed. Madeleine B. Stern (New York: William Morrow, 1975).

"The Skeleton in the Closet," in Perley Parker, *The Foundling* (Boston: Elliott, Thomes & Talbot, [1867]). No. 49 in *Ten Cent Novelettes* series of *Standard American Authors.* Repr. in *Plots and Counterplots,* ed. Madeleine B. Stern (New York: William Morrow, 1976).

"The Abbot's Ghost: or, Maurice Treherne's Temptation," *The Flag of Our Union* (5, 12, 19, and 26 January 1867). Repr. in *Behind a Mask,* ed. Madeleine B. Stern (New York: William Morrow, 1975).

"Hope's Debut," *Frank Leslie's Chimney Corner* (6 April 1867). Repr.

in *Louisa May Alcott: Selected Fiction,* ed. Daniel Shealy, Madeleine B. Stern, and Joel Myerson (Boston: Little, Brown, 1991).

"Thrice Tempted," *Frank Leslie's Chimney Corner* (20 July 1867). Repr. in *Louisa May Alcott: Selected Fiction,* ed. Daniel Shealy, Madeleine B. Stern, and Joel Myerson (Boston: Little, Brown, 1991).

"Taming a Tartar," *Frank Leslie's Illustrated Newspaper* (30 November and 7, 14, and 21 December 1867). Repr. in *A Modern Mephistopheles and Taming a Tartar,* ed. Madeleine B. Stern (New York: Praeger, 1987); and in *A Double Life,* ed. Madeleine B. Stern, Joel Myerson, and Daniel Shealy (Boston: Little, Brown, 1988).

"Doctor Dorn's Revenge," *Frank Leslie's Lady's Magazine* (February 1868). Repr. in this volume.

"La Jeune; or, Actress and Woman," *Frank Leslie's Chimney Corner* (18 April 1868). Repr. in *Freaks of Genius,* ed. Daniel Shealy, Madeleine B. Stern, and Joel Myerson (Westport, Conn.: Greenwood, 1991).

"Countess Varazoff," *Frank Leslie's Lady's Magazine* (June 1868). Repr. in this volume.

"The Romance of a Bouquet," *Frank Leslie's Illustrated Newspaper* (27 June 1868). Repr. in *Freaks of Genius,* ed. Daniel Shealy, Madeleine B. Stern, and Joel Myerson (Westport, Conn.: Greenwood, 1991).

"A Laugh and a Look," *Frank Leslie's Chimney Corner* (4 July 1868). Repr. in *Freaks of Genius,* ed. Daniel Shealy, Madeleine B. Stern, and Joel Myerson (Westport, Conn.: Greenwood, 1991).

"Fatal Follies," *Frank Leslie's Lady's Magazine* (September 1868). Repr. in this volume.

"Fate in a Fan," *Frank Leslie's Lady's Magazine* (January 1869). Repr. in this volume.

"Perilous Play," *Frank Leslie's Chimney Corner* (13 February 1869). Repr. in *Frank Leslie's Popular Monthly* (November 1876); and in *Plots and Counterplots,* ed. Madeleine B. Stern (New York: William Morrow, 1976).

"Which Wins?" *Frank Leslie's Lady's Magazine* (March 1869). Repr. in this volume.

"Honor's Fortune," *Frank Leslie's Lady's Magazine* (June 1869). Repr. in this volume.

"Mrs. Vane's Charade," *Frank Leslie's Chimney Corner* (21 August

1869). Repr. in *Freaks of Genius,* ed. Daniel Shealy, Madeleine B. Stern, and Joel Myerson (Westport, Conn.: Greenwood, 1991).

"My Mysterious Mademoiselle," *Frank Leslie's Lady's Magazine* (September 1869). Repr. in this volume.

"Betrayed by a Buckle," *Frank Leslie's Lady's Magazine* (February 1870). Repr. in this volume.

"La Belle Bayadère," *Frank Leslie's Lady's Magazine* (February 1870). Repr. in this volume.